TALES OF BLOOD AND INK

KATE MACLEOD

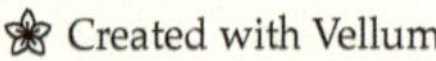 Created with Vellum

CONTENTS

BLOOD AND INK

Morinaga Shiori sighed and shifted her son on her lap. It had been her decision to nurse him, a secret lest the other ladies of Heian-kyo consider her more provincial than they already did, but the never-ending summer heat made it a miserable experience. His sweaty flesh was pressed up against her just when she most longed for nothing touching her but a soft breeze, or perhaps any icy mountain spring like the one back home.

The memory washed over her. She played with the sensations in her mind, and she knew just what brushstrokes she would use to try to convey the coolness of the water, thick to thin and curving just so. She reached for her writing desk to pull it nearer, but her son grunted in complaint and she sat still and let him eat.

Later. She could paint later.

She looked up at the whisper of silk on the polished wood floor and saw her mother hurrying in with her careful steps.

"I will take Yoshi now," she said. "Sakura is here to call on you."

Shiori gently pried her son's mouth off her breast, kissed the top of his hot but soft head, and handed him to his eager grandmother. Then she ran her hands over the many layers of her juni-hito, trying to make them all perfect. The silk was wrinkled from where Yoshi's sweaty body had lain, but at least there were no telltale drops of milk staining the outer layers.

She had just taken up her fan and settled her hands on her lap, getting that Heian-kyo look on her face like she had done nothing all day but wait for someone to call on her, when Sakura came in.

"Good morning, Morinaga Shiori," she said with a bow.

"Good morning, Meiji Sakura," Shiori said. "It's good to see you."

"It's been too long," Sakura said, opening her fan, every angle of her fingers and wrists just so, although there was no one but Shiori to see it. "I'm having a poetry recital tomorrow evening; do tell me you'll come."

"Oh, Sakura, you know I have no skill for poetry," Shiori sighed. She didn't add that she suspected the other ladies were ridiculing what attempts she made behind her back; Sakura would only tell her she was imaging things.

"Perhaps you could show some of your kakemono instead. I'm sure the others wouldn't mind," Sakura said with a pretty flutter of her fan. Shiori was about to answer but was obliged to wait as a servant brought in the sake, setting it on a little table nearby before disappearing once more. Shiori held her tongue as she poured for both of them, trying to hold back the full sleeve of her juni-hito with at least a hint of artfulness. She didn't have Sakura's flair for gestures; she was always in too much of a hurry. Only when Sakura had taken a sip of the sake and gently set down her bowl did Shiori finally speak. "Perhaps you would help me to choose which kakemono to bring to your poetry reading?"

"It would be an honor," Sakura said with a smile. Shiori went across the room to the wood boxes which held all of her tightly rolled scrolls. She dug around only for a moment before she found the two she had painted just the night before and brought them to Sakura.

"Ah, this is your husband, Fujiya Takehiko, no?" Sakura said, fanning herself as she examined the ink portrait. "Did he sit for you to paint this?"

"No, I did it from memory," Shiori said. She did not add that she had not seen Takehiko since shortly after their son was born, seven months ago. She unrolled the second kakemono.

"This is also your husband," Sakura said. Her eyebrows drew down in a slight frown. For once Meiji Sakura did not know the proper thing to say.

"Yes, but they're different. Don't you see?" Shiori asked. Sakura looked from one to the other.

"I confess they seem the same to me, but I am no judge of painting. It is so odd, painting just someone's face like this; I have never seen it done. And why did you do two? Are they to be a matched set?"

"They are different," Shiori said, turning the scrolls in her hands so that she could look upon them. The difference was clear in her eyes: one was Takehiko with fiery passion in his eyes, the other was Takehiko, cold and remote. How had she failed to convey it? But then even with the real Takehiko before her, she couldn't always tell which state he was in until he began to speak.

"Perhaps a painting from nature? I know you could do something lovely," Sakura suggested.

"I was just thinking of a new one," Shiori admitted. "I was thinking of the spring near my home in Nagano. It's been so hot in Heian-kyo, I would love to paint something cool."

"That would be lovely," Sakura said. "Only don't say 'my home in Nagano'. The others may find that too countrified."

"Of course," Shiori said, grateful that the white powder on her face was thick enough to cover the sudden flaming of her cheeks. "Heian-kyo is my home."

"Of course," Sakura smiled and fluttered her fan.

———

Night brought no relief; if anything, it became more stiflingly hot than before. Shiori had set aside her juni-hito, wearing only the sleeveless garment of a peasant - and a male peasant at that - but she needed her arms bare and free to paint. By the flickering light of her candles, she ground her ink stick and mixed it with water until the blue-black pool was the perfect consistency. Then she took up the brush she had left soaking. The bristles were now saturated with no air bubbles trapped within, but there were three hairs that had been bent and refused to lie with the others.

Shiori took her little knife to trim the hairs, but she could not see them against the dark wood of her table by candlelight. She picked up the brush once more, letting it rest against the side of her thumb and gently trimming away the errant bristles.

Yoshi gave a sudden shriek in the still night and Shiori jumped, slicing her own knuckle with the blade. Several drops of blood dripped into her ink before she put her thumb to her mouth, sucking the wound as she went to help her mother calm Yoshi. It was just a little cut; it would not keep her from painting.

It was very late when she at last returned to her work; the candles had burned down low. If she were going to paint this night, she would have to start at once. There was no time to mix fresh ink.

She closed her eyes and put herself back home in Nagano, at her favorite spring. She listened to the chatter of the water dancing over the rocks, the burble as it pooled in the deep places. She felt the chill of the air that followed the water down the mountain and smelled the sharp, sticky aroma of the pine trees that grew along its banks.

She opened her eyes and began to paint.

———

Shiori sipped sake and tried not to look bored. She hated poetry. She knew she missed the nuances that delighted the others; she could not tell a good poem from a bad one. In Nagano there were many ways to pass an evening together, but in Heian-kyo with its insistence on formalities, things were more limited. The screen that separated the women from the eyes of the men divided any party in half and made poetry recitals one of the few entertainment options. One could scarcely play go around a screen that went from floor to ceiling. And her kakemono was still tightly rolled in the corner where Sakura had placed it on Shiori's arrival.

"Greetings, Morinaga Shiori," said a woman whose name Shiori could not recall. Luckily the woman's intent was gossip, not social politeness, so she went on without waiting for Shiori to respond. "I hear Fujiya Takehiko will be here tonight. Is this true?"

"I don't know," Shiori said then was instantly certain that had been the wrong thing to say. Now all of Heian-kyo would know her husband no longer called on her.

"He often attends Meiji Sakura's poetry recitals. He has a fine gift with words, doesn't he?" the woman went on.

"Many seem to think so."

"Meiji Sakura is also a wonderful poet, isn't she? Perhaps this evening the two of them will have a poetry contest like they had a fortnight ago. That was a wonderful time; it's a shame you weren't there! I think Meiji Sakura had the upper hand in the end, but Fujiya Takehiko left determined to best her in the next match." The woman fluttered her fan and gave the falsest of smiles. And then she was gone, to Shiori's immense relief.

"Morinaga Shiori, I think now would be the perfect time to view your kakemono," Sakura announced, and the room was filled with polite murmurs of agreement. Shiori bowed then went to retrieve her scroll. She had scarcely slept last night, for even after she had finished painting the spring, her mind had been alive with sensations she had to commit to paper. She had filled scroll after scroll with twisted trees and stately cranes and dancing fish before at last falling asleep with her elbow in her nearly dry ink well.

She unrolled the kakemono and then turned to show it to the others. Her stomach was rocking like a typhoon, too much anxiety and sake on top of too little food. The women gathered around, their white faces giving no hint to their thoughts. They nodded and made little murmurs, but each was careful not to actually express an opinion until Sakura had decided whether or not the piece was good.

Sakura stepped forward to examine it more closely. Her face was intent as her gaze followed the curving lines of the painting. Then she closed her eyes with a blissful smile.

"Can't you feel it? Oh, it's wonderful. So cool..."

The other women looked at each other nervously. One brave soul drew nearer to stand next to Sakura. For a moment she just continued to fan herself as she stared at the painting, but then the studious look left her face and she too was throwing her head back, loosening the folds of her juni-hito as if to enjoy some breeze only she and Sakura were feeling.

Now all the women were rushing forward, pushing each other aside to stand before Shiori and her scroll. Shiori felt like crying. She knew they didn't like her, but this mockery was really too much. She was just about to throw the kakemono to the ground and leave, no matter how unseemly such behavior would be judged, when a voice carried from beyond the screen.

"May I see your kakemono, Morinaga Shiori?"

So, he had arrived at last.

"Yes. Yes, of course," Shiori said, rolling up the scroll and sliding it under the screen. Takehiko reached out to take it from her, deliberately letting his fingers slide against hers. And her heart did a little leap. At that moment, Shiori would have gladly taken both her leaping heart and typhoon stomach and buried them deeply in the earth. Useless traitorous things.

The women were all laughing and talking together, fanning themselves lazily as if in a languorous mood. Shiori reached for her sake bowl and drained the whole thing in one long swallow. The silence on the other side of the screen was tormenting.

Then there was a happy childlike laugh that she was startled to realize came from Takehiko himself.

"This is divine!" he cried, and one of the other men began to laugh as well.

"How do you do it?" one of the women asked Shiori. "Did you have an onmyoji cast a spell on it for you?"

"No, I just painted it," Shiori said. Her hands were twisting together in her lap, and she realized she was rubbing the cut on the side of her thumb.

Takehiko went home with her after the party and even stayed in the morning to watch little Yoshi play in the garden. He was still there when her father returned home. It was over rice and pickled greens that Takehiko finally made his announcement.

"My father wishes me to take a second wife," he said, his eyes on Shiori although he was speaking to her father.

"Meiji Sakura," she said softly.

"Yes," he admitted. "Her social connections are needful for the progression of my career, my father says."

"Of course we understand," Shiori's mother said. "Shiori is just a provincial girl. She is not much help to you."

"It was my father's idea," Takehiko said, and Shiori saw the fire was back in his eyes. "I will always honor Shiori as my first wife."

"That is very good to hear," Shiori's mother said. She looked intently at her daughter, and Shiori at last realized she was supposed to say something.

"Thank you, Fujiya Takehiko," she said with a bow.

Part of her wondered if he would ever call again now that he had such a fashionable and lively wife. Part of her wondered if she had just lost her only friend now that they would share a husband.

Mostly she was waiting for him to leave so she could get back to painting.

It was nightfall again before she was alone with her ink and paper. She soaked her brush then gently ground her ink stick, all of the rituals of preparation she enjoyed nearly as much as the painting itself. Then, without really thinking to herself what she was doing, she picked up the knife and pricked her thumb, adding several drops of blood to the ink well.

She closed her eyes and imagined a plum tree. What brushstrokes would show the silkiness of the plum blossoms? What would convey the hum of the bees overhead, the roughness of the bark, the sweetness of the fruit? The imagined brushstrokes flowed through her mind, curling and spiraling, growing thick and dark then thin and watery. This one meant the purple tartness of a plum; that one was the blue splutter of a dragonfly's wings.

She painted.

———

The heat faded and summer gave way to autumn. Yoshi could pull himself up on the edge of her writing table and toddle about, tugging at his mother's long hair as she bent over any of an endless stream of scrolls. She would smile at him, tickle his chin or kiss his fat cheek, but only for a moment. Then she was back in the painting. She could not paint fast enough to keep up with her racing thoughts, and there was so much in her head that she had to get out.

Sakura had indeed become Takehiko's second wife, but Shiori didn't care much. The two of them made sure she had all of the ink and paper and brushes she could possibly need. They also made sure that all of Heian-kyo stood in front of Shiori's kakemono to experience her unique art. Takehiko had even written a poem about her painting, about how one's eyes followed the curves and angles of her brush-strokes and suddenly one was tasting plums or hearing the mournful call of the crane.

Shiori didn't go to the parties anymore. She still wasn't entirely sure that all of Heian-kyo society wasn't playing some elaborate cruel joke on her. And yet it was for Heian-kyo society that she painted, to show them the value of the rest of the world, the provincial world they had such disdain for. She hadn't accomplished that yet. Although her kakemono were in great demand and every fashionable home had to have one or two hanging from its walls, no one had yet gone out to experience the real thing.

Her parents would not look at her kakemono or allow her to hang any of them from the walls of their home. She seldom saw her father, gone as he was most of the day, but her mother was a constant presence, nagging that Yoshi needed feeding, or Shiori's hair needed washing, and just where was she getting all of these cuts?

Shiori stopped cutting her hands to get blood for her ink. She also stopped painting in peasant's garb, wearing her oldest juni-hito instead. She did not tie the long sleeves back, she just let them drag about as they would, and soon they were blotched all over with deep blue-black ink.

Autumn was beginning to turn to winter when her mother made a most unwelcome suggestion.

"I want you to stop painting."

Shiori sat back on her heels, uncertain at first that she had heard correctly. When she was caught up in the world in her head, the world outside her head came through distorted or not at all.

"Why?" she asked at last. Her mother reached out and pulled back one of Shiori's sleeves, exposing a forearm criss-crossed with cuts old and new, the newer ones longer and deeper.

"It's nothing," Shiori said, smoothing the ink-stained sleeve back into place.

"It is, I think, why the others love your kakemono so much," her mother said. "Because of what you put into them from yourself. But even the most glorious kakemono is still just ink on paper. I don't wish to watch you fade away before my eyes. I don't wish to be left with nothing but ink on paper."

"I am well, mother," Shiori insisted, although she knew that wasn't true. She was tired, so tired, and yet she could not sleep.

"Shiori, you are a good mother. A better mother than I was at your age. I don't think I even spoke to you until you were six or seven. Too busy going to poetry recitals and perfume parties. Ah, to be fifteen again! But you've never done such things. I know you love Yoshi. He loves you too, but he misses you. Even when you're with him, you're not really there."

"I know," Shiori said. "But I have to finish this. I'm working towards something, I can feel it. Do you remember when Yoshi was born? My pains started in the evening and went all night then all day and into the evening again. All of these things I've been painting, they've been like those labor pains, a necessary process to work through but not the true purpose. I'm close to the end. I don't know what it's going to be, but when it happens, it will be sublime."

Her mother sat quietly for several long minutes before speaking once more. "When you have painted this last great kakemono, then you will stop?"

"Yes, for there will be no more reason to paint," Shiori said.

That night the brushstrokes would not come. She had painted all she could think of over the last few months, every bird and tree and mountain she had ever seen. What was left to paint? What was still burning in her mind, what experience did she still need to convey to the people of Heian-kyo?

Should she try again to capture the subtleties of Takehiko's moods in a portrait? But the idea held no appeal for her any longer. Takehiko had moved on, and she had no feelings on the matter, ill or otherwise.

Then she knew, she knew what to paint in a rush of inspiration that left her weak and trembling, dizzier than after the strongest sake, more vibrant than after the most passionate night in her husband's arms.

She closed her eyes. Warm, sweet smell. That perfect size to hold in your arms, small enough to cuddle but big and plump enough to squeeze without worry. Tiny fingers always inexplicably sticky. The musical tones of his wordless voice.

The perfect brushstrokes lit up like a fire in her mind; she only copied them. Stroke after stroke, scroll after scroll she painted. Her ink well went dry and she mixed more, then more, then more again.

Yoshi, she thought, as the fire in her mind spread through her body and she began to melt. Here is Yoshi.

Her mother found her there in the morning, laying on stacks of kakemono, each one painted with ink a bit more brownish-red and less blue than the one before. Her paintbrush was still clutched in one scarred hand, and there was a smile of perfect peace on her face.

OIL FIRE

f I had been a child of one of the twelve great Houses, my crime of stealing scrolls from the priests' library would have been punishable by death. My body would have been left atop my House's tower until my flesh filled the bellies of the sentinel birds, then my picked-clean bones placed in the city walls so that in death I would still serve a purpose, warding the city from the demonic vapors that swept down from the mountains at night and filled the river valley all around Ummur's walls. Not even the humblest goatherd dared remain outside the city's walls past moonrise.

But I was not a child of a great House. My death would serve no purpose, but I could not be tolerated to live among the chosen. So I was banished. I walked down the dusty road south of Ummur, the priests watching every step I took until the road dipped out of sight.

But I was back within the walls well before moonrise, using the knowledge I had "stolen" from the priests to hide from the guards' sight. There was more in their library I needed to know before I could leave Ummur.

As I skirted around the marketplace filled with farmers and artisans setting out their goods I wondered if that was still true. There were a few scrolls left which I had never read, in the library off limits to all but the highest ranking priests, but I would have to face great risk to get to them. Perhaps it was time to move on, to follow my clues to the city of the goddess far to the north. I was certain I could find it, if only I had the courage to take the first step outside the walls of my city.

Those walls towered over me as I neared the hiding place I called home. It was the blood and the bones of the members of the great Houses, the descendents of the city's twelve founders, which the priests said had the protective magic that kept the vapors without, but as with all things magic the common people believed there was power in imitation. So within the mighty walls and watchtowers of Ummur there was another humbler wall, a row of former homes and shops now given over as abodes to the dead so that the common folk could feel that their ancestors too were guarding them. It was unthinkable that a sentinel bird should be tempted to eat profane flesh, so the rooms containing the bodies were sealed, windows and doors. Airy mud brick homes became ovens in the hot summer, and the smell of slow-roasting flesh hung thick in the air. No one lingered needlessly in the neighborhoods of the dead. It was the perfect hiding place.

Being banished had served me well. No longer needing to spend my days among the sisters keeping the temple, now I studied until weariness took me, then woke to study again. Soon I would know all the priests knew. Only then would I allow myself to be banished from Ummur, to go out into the world and find more knowledge than the priests could ever dream of.

That had been my plan. But one hot summer day I woke to the sound of a funeral procession, the clatter of tambourines and sistrums and the wailing song of the dancers. The procession was passing on the main road that ran from the ziggurat at the heart of the city out to the watchtower for the House Elam. I saw the number of dancers who were employed in singing and scattering wilted flower petals, the finery of the mourners' clothing, and the ornate bier being used to carry the veiled body of the deceased, and I realized they were not bound for any of my neighbors' houses; they were going to climb the tower itself, the tower of House Elam.

Oh, poor Enanatuma, my sister in all but blood! This could only mean her father, the head of House Elam, was dead. Her father, who had welcomed me, his daughter's strange orphan friend of no House, her fellow temple dancer, into his home. He who had given me the most important gift of all when he had shown me how to read, to unlock the mysteries of the library it was my tiresome duty to keep clean. Her father was gone, and her House would need a new head.

I watched the procession go by from the shadows of an alley. They were close enough to touch; some of the dancers' skirts brushed against me as they passed by. I had to be that close to see their faces, to see Enanatuma as she passed. I only realized my voice had joined that of the dancers when a woman's head turned my way, eyes searching but not finding me. I bit my lip to keep myself silent and pulled my veil closer around me. The veil had jewels that hung over my forehead, the largest one in the middle positioned over the blue tattoo that marked me an outcast from Ummur. That was a bit of cheek on my part; in truth that enspelled jewel hid more than the mark from view. The moment its cool facets touched my skin I could not be seen; I did not even cast a shadow.

A familiar face passed by, Enanatuma's cousin Amar-Sin. I had never known him well, had only seen him a few times waiting to walk Enanatuma home from the temple. The years had not been kind to him. Some great pain, some frustrated longing was etched on his face. It was too much to be for his uncle; the furrows it had left in his face were too old. He walked alone, no wife at his side, no children around him. He was a noble son, so it was unthinkable that he wouldn't marry. It was nearly unthinkable that he wouldn't marry again if his first wife had died without bearing him children, but surely that must be the case.

Enanatuma and her family walked at the end of the procession. Her husband Shulgi carried their little daughter in his arms and held their son by the hand. Enanatuma looked pale and confused, as if she hadn't yet realized what was happening. I fell into step beside her and slipped my arm through hers, giving her hand a squeeze. She stopped walking, letting the procession carry on without her.

"Puabi?" she whispered. "Is it really you?"

"Yes," I whispered back. We had been estranged long before my banishment. I had seen her only once since the day ten years ago when I had given up dancing and devoted all my energies to magic. I had done her a favor in return for the thousand kindnesses she and her father had shown me and had intended never to see her again. But she was still my sister, and judging from the light in her eyes at the sound of my voice, I was still hers.

"I need you," she said. I couldn't tell from her words whether it was Puabi her sister or Puabi worker of magic that she needed, but either way I had only one answer to give.

"I shall come. Tonight." I got up on tiptoe to kiss her cheek, for she was tall, with arms that didn't come from spinning and weaving. Which goes to show that sometimes people don't need my spells to fail to see the obvious. "My heart weeps with yours, sister."

"I know," she murmured back. Then she was gone, running to retake her place at Shulgi's side. He turned to look back. The last time I had seen him he had been dressed in someone else's cast-off rags and covered with brick dust, and I had thought him the finest looking man in all Ummur. Ten years of easy living had softened him, but only a bit, and the violet robes of a noble son suited him more than I had ever dreamed they would. I found I could not turn away; I had to take this moment of seeing him that I had so diligently denied myself for so long.

I think his dark eyes almost saw me even through the spell, his gaze was so intent, but then his daughter tugged his hair sharply and he turned away.

———

Enanatuma and I had been terrible dancers. We both loved the movements and the feeling of being in motion, but we never had the proper reverence to the gods, which was the first calling of a temple dancer, or so Sister Nata had told us over and over. This was perfectly true. Neither of us wanted to learn to use our bodies to honor the gods. I used my dancer's grace and strength to run from rooftop to rooftop across Ummar, vaulting garden walls and climbing to tantalizingly forbidden rooms. Enanatuma used hers to practice the art of gis-gis-la.

Her father teaching me, a girl, to read had been a grievous sin. But it paled in comparison to teaching his daughter the gis-gis-la. I knew from the ancient scrolls that once all had practiced the gis-gis-la, but over time it had been restricted to just members of the twelve Great Houses, and then to just the men. If it were ever known that Enanatuma's father had taught her this martial art, their entire House would be put to death, from the members of the House council to the lowliest cousin of a cousin, and their watchtower and the city walls containing the bones of their ancestors razed to the ground lest the demonic vapors take advantage of the weakness such a sin represented.

It was still a danger to the rest of the House even now that he was dead, which was why I was not surprised to find Enanatuma's house empty of servants as I slipped over the garden wall. I could hear the clang of blade on blade as she drilled with her husband. No servant could be trusted to keep such a secret, especially not considering which of them was the student and which the teacher.

I lingered in the garden, waiting for them to finish and Shulgi to leave. I had often watched Enanatuma practice the gis-gis-la with her father, mastering the spins and leaps, slashing away with her long-bladed sword and catching her opponent's blade with the prongs on the hilt of her dagger.

She had gotten very good since I had last watched her fight. Shulgi was clumsy and slow by comparison. At last he gave up with a curse, throwing the blades to the floor and storming out of the room.

I felt a cold chill in my heart. This was not the Shulgi I had once known so well.

Enanatuma fetched up the blades and set them reverently in their place of honor around the family altar. Enanatuma had just bowed her head in prayer when she twitched at the sound of my sandaled feet on the stone floor. I tugged off my veil and her face lit up briefly before darkening once more, as if she wanted to smile and burst into tears both at once.

"Sister," I said. "What ails Shulgi?"

"Oh, he--" But the tears at last came and it was several minutes before she could continue. I held her close, as once upon a time she had held me, and waited to hear how I would be needed.

"It is as you feared," she said at last. "He truly believes he is a noble son of House Akitu. So he gets angry when he cannot fight the gis-gis-la as any noble son can do, and he will not listen to my advice on how to conduct House business."

"With your father dead, he is head of House Elam?" Enanatuma had no uncles, no close family at all, only distant cousins. But they were cousins very covetous of power.

"Only until Eku comes of age," Enanatuma said, "but yes."

"What do you need me to do?" Ten years ago I had not appreciated that magic raged like an oil fire. If one were not careful it would grow too hot too fast, and trying to douse it would only spread it more. I had learned more control since I had crafted that spell for Enanatuma, one that made everyone believe Shulgi was a long lost son of Akitu, but at the time I had had more confidence than skill. The spell had worked, but it was as though I had used too much oil for such a small spell. It made a flame that was higher and hotter than needed for the task. I could not extinguish that flame; I could only try to keep it from spreading further.

"I don't want you to undo it," Enanatuma said.

"He will go deeper," I warned. "Soon he will realize he should not allow you to practice the gis-gis-la. What then?"

"Then I give up the gis-gis-la," she said.

I did not believe her. For her to put up her blades would be like me giving up magic; it was unthinkable. But there were still tears in her eyes, and I didn't have the heart to argue with her.

"What is it you need?" I asked.

"Help Shulgi. Help him to be a good head of House Elam, and keep him safe. I fear my cousins are watching him closely, waiting for him to make even the smallest misstep. Particularly Amar-Sin."

"Amar-Sin wants to rule your House?" I recalled the man I had seen that morning, wrought with grief. I found it difficult to imagine him conspiring to do anything.

"Sometimes I think so," Enanatuma said. "Sometimes I think he suspects Shulgi is not what he claims to be. He almost seems to hate him, although I don't know how that could be."

"Has he changed since his wife died?"

"What? Amar-Sin never married."

"Never married?" Then why the grief?" But Enanatuma was already impatient with me.

"Please, can you help Shulgi?"

"I confess, I do not know any spells to make him a great leader, but at the very least I can make a protective charm to shield him from poisons and magical attacks."

"Thank you, Puabi."

———

It took me longer than I had anticipated to make the charm, an armband of gold studded with assorted gemstones. Each gem was the focus of its own protective spell; in truth every such spell I knew. If there were anyone in the world who wanted Shulgi kept safe more than Enanatuma did, it was me. The individual spells were easy enough, but finding a way to mount them on the gold band so that they created harmony took a little more work.

And so it was three nights later when I came to bring it to Enanatuma. I was quite proud of it, the most complex magic I had ever worked, but the moment I saw her stricken face I knew I was too late.

"He has been challenged," she said dully. "He ignored my advice about how to conduct House business and has offended Amar-Sin, who was looking to be offended, like as not. Now my cousin has the excuse he was looking for and has called Shulgi out."

"Amar-Sin is good at gis-gis-la?"

"One of the best, by reputation," she said. "Not that it matters; a 10-year-old boy could beat Shulgi, and he knows it. He will not speak to me about it at all, only keeps drinking bowl after bowl of date wine."

The challenge would be a fight to the death. Worse, the victor would control the fate of the defeated's family. Amar-Sin would as good as own Enanatuma, and her children could be cast from their home or banished from Ummur entirely at his whim. If he were feeling particularly vindictive, he could have young Ekar executed to ensure he never sought revenge for his father.

The words were out of my mouth before the thought even entered my mind: "Could you beat him?"

Enanatuma looked surprised, then thoughtful. "Yes," she said at last. "Yes, I could."

"The challenge is at dawn?"

"Yes. At the square before the ziggurat."

"I need a piece of jewelry, something you can wear under gis-gis-la armor."

Enanatuma nodded and pulled a long necklace from around her neck. It was a simple thing, an imperfect piece of lapis lazuli tied to a cord of leather. It had been tucked unseen under her gown. The lapis lazuli was still warm from her flesh.

"Shulgi's first gift to me," she said. I nodded, not trusting myself to speak. I knew the piece well; I had worn it myself for just one night before it was ever Enanatuma's.

"When I am finished with this, it will disguise you. You will look like Shulgi, but you won't sound like him," I said. "Can you do this?"

"Yes. It will be tricky, but there is no ritual which says I must speak."

"It would be best to keep the fight brief." She rolled her eyes at me, just for an instant like her younger self as scornful of me telling her how to fight the gis-gis-la as I would be of her telling me how to cast a spell. Then she was serious once more.

"I will tell the servants I am going to the temple to pray for his victory in case they should notice my absence," she said. "But what about Shulgi?"

"I will see to Shulgi," I promised.

There was scarcely enough time for me to cross the city to my room, imbue the stone with the spell, and then carry it back across the ever-brightening city to Enanatuma's house. She was anxiously awaiting my return, casting nervous glances at Shulgi's form on their low bed. She was already dressed in his armor, which needed only a little padding around the shoulders and waist to fit her.

"He will wake soon. He had a lot of wine, but even so, he is always an early riser," she said.

"He will remain here with me until the fight is done; you can trust me on that." I slipped the leather cord over her head, tucking the stone beneath the breastplate. Then I looked up into Shulgi's dark eyes and my breath caught.

"I just thought," Enanatuma said, her voice snapping me out of my reverie. "I will always be Shulgi when I wear this now, won't I?"

"Yes," I said. "The spell will not fade, and it cannot be broken." I wondered for the first time what dangerous power I had just given her. But she was my most trusted sister; I kissed her cheek and let her go.

I sat with my back against one of the pillars that divided Enanatuma's bedroom from the garden beyond and waited for Shulgi to wake. The sun was not yet over the garden wall, but the air was already still and hot. I imagined Enanatuma fighting in that metal armor in the shadeless square before the ziggurat. No wonder challenges were always met at dawn.

Shulgi had passed out draped facedown across the bed, still dressed in his formal garb from the House council meeting that had led to the challenge. This close to him, I could see the strands of silver just beginning to show in his still-thick hair. My hand itched to touch it, to see if the waves of it were as soft as I remembered.

This would be the hardest part. I had not spoken to him since the morning so many years ago when I had left him alone in our makeshift bed with only the lapis lazuli necklace on the pillow beside him. I hadn't trusted myself. Now I would have to speak to him, to keep him here until Enanatuma returned. Worse, I had to let him speak to me and not search his every word, every tone, for clues to his true thoughts. The past must stay in the past.

At last he began to stir, groaning and rubbing at his face. Then he saw the sunbeam nearly touching his hand and remembered.

He jumped up from the bed, sober and alert in the blink of an eye, and rushed towards the cedar chest that held his gis-gis-la armor, or had before Enanatuma had taken it.

"Shulgi," I called softly just as his hand touched the lid. He spun, eyes searching the garden before at last falling upon me.

"Puabi?" He had a strange look to his face, as if he had just spoken a name he had heard once and had no idea whether it was connected to me or not. A look of recognition almost washed over his face but retreated just as rapidly.

"It is I," I said simply. "Puabi." Was it the mere affirmation of his confusing suspicions that brought that look of recognition back, or was it the sound of my voice? Whatever the cause, his eyes lit up and I knew he knew me.

"I searched everywhere for you!"

"I know it."

"I went every day to the temple in hopes of seeing you."

"So I gave up being a dancer."

"Why?" There was no need to search the tones of that word for meaning; it was filled with pain and loss that could not be hidden.

"You know why."

But I wondered if he did anymore. He believed himself a noble son; believed it mind, heart and soul. How would he remember our time together, I an orphaned ward of the temple sisters, he a refugee from a far-off city who had found work repairing the high city walls of Ummur, dangerous work with little pay. Neither of us much better than slaves. How could we marry with no money for a home, no money to feed children?

And yet I had convinced myself that it was possible. I had accepted his proposal and his gift, the lapis lazuli necklace which had been his mother's; it was all he had to give. I would have married him, I know I would have, if my sleep that night hadn't been disturbed by the wail of a child.

I had left Shulgi's side, crawled to the edge of our hiding place on the roof of a shop near the temple. It was the perfect place to sleep on hot summer nights. From my vantage point I saw a woman laying a squalling infant on the temple steps, just as I had been left so many years before. She kissed the baby, wiped at her eyes, then hurried away.

Another child waited for her in the shadows of an alley, a boy of six or seven years. She took his hand, and after one last long look back at the babe she was gone.

What had happened? The child on the steps was a baby, but not newly born. Some change in this woman's circumstance meant she could no longer feed both children, I surmised, but what? Had something happened to her husband?

A sudden vision filled my mind: Shulgi falling from the city walls to be dashed on the rocky ground below.

I didn't know what had happened to that woman; I only knew I could never be her.

I wasn't certain how much Shulgi remembered beyond my name. He looked confused, his eyes washing over me and then looking around the room and then back at me. His past and his present didn't seem to connect in his mind.

He would never know what I had done for him, how I had made sure he and Enanatuma would meet. Noble daughter that she was, she had money enough for both of them. She could keep him safe. She was the one person I knew who would raise him up from his lowly place in the world, who would see what he could be and not just what he was. And he had been perfect for her, he would never try to make Enanatuma a meek woman, touching only spindles and looms. He would love her as she was.

So he would have, had I never cast that spell.

Enanatuma never realized what I had done, either, to bring them together. How nervous she was, the day she asked me to weave the spell that would make him a noble son, the little difference between a man she could marry and one she could not. I hadn't even needed a jewel to focus the spell on, only a scrap of paper, a genealogy of House Akitu that could hold a few extra "long-lost" branches. I gave Shulgi an ancestor so I could give him to Enanatuma.

He was still staring at me, confused. Then he looked down at his hand resting on the cedar chest.

"Shulgi!" I said, stepping forward, but too late. He had already thrown back the lid and was staring at the empty space where his armor should be.

"What's going on?" he asked. "Where is Enanatuma?"

"She is saving your life and her House. Be still and let her do it."

"What do you know of my wife?" he demanded.

"Think of your children. Think of Eku. This was the only way," I said.

"What was the only way? And what do you know of my children? Why are you even here, now?" Then I saw his eyes move up to my forehead, to the blue mark the priests had tattooed there. "You were banished. Why?"

Before I could answer, Shulgi's eyes moved past me to the garden and a look of shock froze his features. I turned to see his mirror image in dusty armor clutching a blood-soaked cloth to the side of his face.

"What happened?" I cried.

"I was victorious," Enanatuma said, "but I paid a price." And she pulled the cloth away from her Shulgi-face to reveal a gash starting near the corner of her mouth and extending up into her hairline, just missing an eye.

"Oh no," I said, looking from her to her husband and his unmarked cheek.

"What have you done?" he asked, a whisper which held all the urgency of a scream. He dropped onto the edge of the bed, hands clutching violently at his hair.

"What you could not," she said. There was no hint of accusation in her words, only her own fierce brand of love. She gave me the bloody rag and pulled the necklace off over her head. She was Enanatuma once more, but the injury remained.

"It's not serious, sister," I said, for the bleeding had already stopped. "It will heal."

"It will leave a scar," Enanatuma said. "A scar on my face, not Shulgi's."

We must cut him. And yet I couldn't bring myself to say the words aloud. Even if we gave him the scar he lacked, how to explain Enanatuma's? More magic, more illusions?

Ten years had taught me nothing; I was still spreading oil fire even as I tried to douse it.

Shulgi lifted his head from his hands. Enanatuma stood over him, her gis-gis-la dagger in her hand. Her thoughts had followed mine, but she too shirked away from the inevitable. She lowered her arm.

"What you have done has damned every soul in this city," he said to her. "You can cover it up from the eyes of men, perhaps, but not from the eyes of the gods. The wards of House Elam, how will they hold out the demons now that you have done this thing?"

"The same as they have these last twenty years, since I first took up the swords," Enanatuma said.

"How did I allow it?" He was genuinely confused to the point of anguish. Did he remember nothing of his former life?

"No one knows what the vapors are or why the walls keep them out," I said. "The priests act confident, but I've read their most secret texts. They don't really know."

But Shulgi only grew more enraged, leaping to his feet to pace the room. "Do not tell me this was no sin! You who are not one of us, not one of the noble Houses; you don't know what it is to hold this sacred trust that protects us all. To keep the magic in our bones strong throughout life so that they will serve their purpose after death. But Enanatuma knows." And he turned on her. "She knew the sin of it every time she took up the blades. She felt it in her bones. Every time."

Enanatuma met his gaze steadily, saying nothing, but I saw the glint of a tear in her eye and realized there was truth in what he said. I had broken every law of Ummur in my pursuit of knowledge, but I had never once felt I was doing wrong. I had never felt guilt.

But Enanatuma had, and she had never said a word, not even to me, her closest sister.

"You have to leave," Shulgi said at last, and there were tears in both their eyes now. "Leave Ummur. There will be no covering this up, no more illusions, no more tricks."

"Shulgi," I said, but I was unheard.

"You should die, we should all die," he said to her. "It's the law."

"Shulgi, the children-" Enanatuma said.

"Not just our children," he interrupted. "Every child of House Elam will be condemned, and what then? The priests say the walls containing Elam's bones must be razed. The walls of the Houses to either side must be extended to fill the gap. Do you know how long it would take to build those walls? How far we have to go to quarry the stones?" He broke off, a far-off look to his eyes, as if he were trying to recall the details of a dream he had had long ago. "I know," he said and looked down at his hands, as though a part of him expected to find calluses there.

He broke himself out of his reverie with a shake of his head. "And I've spoken only of the stones, not what lies between, what really keeps us all safe. How many would die each night before Ummur was made whole again? Not just our children."

Enanatuma's face contracted as she fought the tears. The gash on her cheek began to bleed anew.

"What else can I do, Enanatuma?" he asked. "What else? I cannot undo what you did. I can only hope your actions have not dishonored us to the point where the gods no longer smile on House Elam." He grabbed her arms now, pulling her close. "You should die for this, I know. But I can't condemn you. Even to save us all, I can't. So you must leave and never return, and be as dead to all Ummur."

"I will go," Enanatuma said. "If Puabi swears to watch over my children, to protect them for me until they are grown and wed."

"How can she, marked as she is? She could never be seen with them," Shulgi said.

"Puabi knows what I am asking," Enanatuma said.

I nodded, and in so doing sealed my fate. It would be years now before I could leave Ummur. Enanatuma hugged me a little too tightly before turning back to Shulgi. "May I say farewell to the children?"

"No," Shulgi said. "My love, your injury. They can't see it, can never know what you've done. We cannot force them to keep such secrets."

"What will you tell them?"

"I don't know. What will I tell anyone?"

"She fled," I said, my words sounding dull in my own ears. "She was certain you would lose, that you would leave her at the mercy of Amar-Sin, who hates her."

Shulgi barked out a laugh that almost sounded self-mocking.

"What?" I asked.

"Amar-Sin does not hate Enanatuma. Quite the opposite. Exactly the opposite."

"What are you talking about?" Enanatuma asked, barely more than a whisper.

"He told me once. It was at our wedding feast. He pulled me aside and told me that you and he had made a vow, that when he returned from his journey to the south the two of you would marry. It was a secret vow, not one sworn before a priest as such things are meant to be done. Don't you remember? I told you about it and you laughed it off as some ridiculous story in his imagination."

"I don't remember," Enanatuma said, but her face had gone very white.

"He's never mentioned it again, but in every look he gives me, in every word he utters, he makes sure I never forget. No, he does not hate you."

Whatever more was going to be said remained unspoken as we heard voices from across the garden and the footfalls of a servant approaching.

"You were seen leaving the fight with rude haste, ignoring many well-wishers. You will need to make apologies and explanations to keep your allies," Enanatuma said. "And if I am gone, you will need those allies more than ever."

Shulgi looked at her, and I could see that he still wrestled with the obligation to surrender his family for the good of the city. I stepped up, pressing the blood-soaked cloth into his hand and raising it to his unshaven cheek.

"Not good enough," Shulgi said, pushing away the cloth and taking the dagger from Enanatuma's hand. One fierce motion and his decision was irrevocably made. Enanatuma tore the cloth from my hand to press it to his cheek, but he pushed her away, knocking her to the floor behind the bed. Then he caught my arm and threw me down beside her.

"Stay down," he hissed, slamming the lid down on the empty armor chest just as the servant appeared.

"What is it?" Shulgi asked.

"Guests, my lord."

"Now? Damn, but this gash is bleeding again."

"Shall I fetch a surgeon, my lord?"

"Why bother? The blood is what they're all here to see," Shulgi said. Enanatuma and I watched as the sandaled feet of the servant left the room, then Shulgi's followed. He had not even said farewell to his wife.

We got to our feet, Enanatuma looking more than a little dazed. "I killed him."

"You had to kill him," I said, reaching for my veil.

"I think what Shulgi said might be true. I think I remember, like a dream I had long ago, making that vow. And we...." She broke off, eyes gazing off into the distance. "Do you remember him?"

"Not at all," I confessed.

"Did I love Amar-Sin once, and *forget*? I abandoned him for Shulgi and forgot every moment we ever had together?"

"Enanatuma...."

"I felt something when he died. I had stabbed him with my parry blade; we were quite close at the end, practically in an embrace. Puabi, I thought at first that he had seen through your spell, because my name was the last word from his lips. Except the way he said it, it brought back such feelings in me. It felt so familiar. I did love him once, didn't I? If I had I would've told you, my sister. Don't you remember?"

"No, you never told me any such thing."

"Can you get caught up in your own spell?"

I could not answer. Enanatuma was desperate to know if she had broken faith with one betrothed to take up with another. I was certain to spend the rest of my life questioning whether I had broken that betrothal myself to bring Shulgi into her life. It was also possible that Amar-Sin's story was truly just his imagination, or something he invented to try to raise his position in House Elam. But was it possible that the spell I had cast to give Shulgi a noble line had not been my first spell on his behalf? Had I first done something to get rid of Amar-Sin?

I would never know. Magic was truly oil fire; it had spread and spread until even I was burned. The spell meant to save the life of my love had led to my dearest sister killing her own lover. I knew in my soul that it was true. Admitting it would give no comfort to my sister, though. All she had left now were memories of her husband, and I wouldn't do anything to poison them.

"You will forget again," I promised her. "Think only of Shulgi and your love for him, and you will forget these other ghosts of memories. But now it's time for you to leave. Take my veil."

I draped it over her and she vanished from sight. Her strong arms pulled me into one last hug and then she was gone.

I would never see her again, never hear of how she fared or whether she even still lived. Would she ever put the necklace on, I wondered, just to look at the reflection of her husband's face in a bronze mirror or a still pond?

As the hot day dragged on, I fell asleep on Enanatuma's bed. It was well past sunset when Shulgi shook me awake. A surgeon had indeed been by, as a row of coarse stitches adorned his cheek. He had cut himself more deeply than Enanatuma had been wounded, but I doubted any but the three of us would ever know the difference. Just two of us now.

"You knew Enanatuma. You were both dancers, sisters at the temple," he said.

"Yes."

"I forgot about you when I married Enanatuma. Not willfully, not like a man putting aside thoughts of an old love for the sake of the new. I forgot you, completely."

"Shulgi," I said, desperately not wanting to have this conversation. "You've forgotten many things."

"They've been coming back since this morning. It's like the story of my life is actually two stories, and I remember them both. They both seem equally true. I'm not sure which *is* true."

"I am sorry."

"Why?"

"Because it was my spell that...." Broke you? Is driving you mad? "It's my fault."

"Yours and Enanatuma's, yes? The two of you plotting together and never once speaking of any of this to me!" He paced again, the violet robes snapping around him in sympathy to his growing fury.

"It was to keep you safe. Everything I did was because I couldn't bear the thought of you dying."

"You made my life a lie!" He turned to face me, and there was something deliberate about the space he left between us. "I have many hateful things to say to you, to you and my now departed wife. How you used me; how you played with me, just another doll in some girls' game."

"No–"

"I won't say them. I choose not to. If I even still have a choice. Enanatuma is gone, now I want you gone as well."

"I cannot leave Ummur," I said. "I promised to watch over your children."

"I will not see you," he said, spitting out the words. "Ever. I will not once ask myself if I'm not secretly pleased that she is gone and you remain. I will not wonder if that was even your intention from the first."

"Shulgi, I never–"

"Go!" he roared, his face so contorted with rage I feared for his stitches.

So I left.

————

I watch over them still, he and the children both. He found the armband I had made for him; I have seen him wearing it. It had been left in Enanatuma's clothes chest; he must have taken it to be a last gift for him that she had never had a chance to give. The children have wards as well, spells imbued in pretty little stones they just happened to find lying in their path and picked up and kept, as children are wont to do.

I wondered what Shulgi thought of it all. I wondered if he would forget me once more, as his past as a noble son would once more become "true" for him, matching his present life as his past as a builder of walls did not.

And sometimes, as I lay in the heat of the day waiting for sleep to take me, I wondered if he had been right about my intentions, and whether he ever did think about me in Enanatuma's place. And I would admit at last, now that it was too late, that it had never truly been the priests' library that had kept me in Ummur after my banishment.

Then I would go to sleep in my little room among the rotting dead, waiting for the day when Enanatuma's children would be grown and I would be free to leave Ummur. Waiting, and fearing when the time came I would find I could not go, and I would linger on to be near to the man who would not see me. Me, the only true ghost in Ummur.

GARDENS OF WIND

The call was raised that the *Parjanya* had been spotted approaching from the nor'east. There was an outcry among the women for all of the last minute tasks that still remained to be done, but Akeli slipped away before her mother could assign her some duty. She knew this wasn't her father's ship approaching, nor her Brandon's ship either, but she still wanted to see it for herself before it docked. She climbed up between the hydroponics rafts to the catwalks that ran over the top of everything. She could still be seen through the glass roofs, but the gardens below were empty, all necessary chores finished early in anticipation of the arrival of the *Parjanya* and the festival to follow.

Akeli reached the end of the al-Khátún and leaned over the railing as far as she dared. The sky was clear, except of course for below, but still she could not see the *Parjanya*. She followed the rail to the balloon rigging, climbing to the very top. There was no rail here, no safety line, nothing between her and a fall to the earth far below save the grip of her hands on the rope ladder. She felt a twinge in her stomach she supposed was fear; that never used to be there. She crept forward, her hands and knees pushing down on the balloon silk without quite letting her sink in.

She had nearly reached the point when the balloon silk descended once more when at last she saw it. It was a proper airship, sure enough, not a lashed together mess of rafts and balloons like the al-Khátún. You could go anywhere you wanted in such a ship, not simply float at the whims of the wind. You could descend below the cloud cover in such a ship without crashing. You could even land on the surface.

Those on crew duty were gathering at the rails below her, ready to toss and catch guidelines to make the *Parjanya* fast and help her people board their floating village. Akeli climbed back down the balloon, avoiding the crew by climbing down through the gap between two rafts as she and Kahlil had done since they were little more than toddlers, climbing like monkeys in a children's story under everyone's unsuspecting feet. They had never once been caught at it, although Akeli supposed if they had her bottom would still be blistered to this day. She paused for a moment, swinging her head far back to look towards the earth below her, lost under the clouds of brown and gray. Her arms soon tired, so she continued on until she reached the hydroponics raft nearest the room she shared with her mother. She slipped inside but realized just as the door shut behind her that she was not alone.

Fortunately the arguing voices had not noticed the rush of wind or the click of the shutting door from the far side of the room. Akeli crouched under the cucumber plants, moving quickly and quietly away from the door just in case one of them had noticed but hadn't said anything.

Then she recognized the voices: her mother and her uncle Hyman, who was the captain of their vessel, such as it was, and the chieftain of their village. Akeli briefly considered sneaking back out the way she'd came, for she knew without even bothering to listen just what they would be fighting about at this auspicious moment, but she doubted she'd get lucky enough to pass unnoticed twice. She crept behind the tool cabinet, dangling tomato plants covering her like a curtain, and waited.

"She just needs time," her mother was saying.

"She's had time. It's been nearly a year," her uncle replied. "I am not without sympathy, sister. She may very well grieve the rest of her life and I will think no less of her. But she can grieve and do her duty as well."

"I don't think she can. She took so long to find her Brandon-"

"All the more reason not to indulge her in long choosing this time around. In the end, it made her no happier letting her have her way."

"Hyman!"

"Well, it's true," her uncle said gruffly, although there was an undertone of contrition in his voice. Not that he would ever admit to feeling it; it was inconceivable that one such as he should apologize to his little sister even for the cruelest of words. "We must look to the future. We cannot survive if there are too few of us, and if every woman's son leaves us, who will care for us in our old age?"

"Our daughters."

"Oh, indeed."

"My son will return," her mother said in a very small voice.

"It is long past time you and Akeli gave up that dream," her uncle said. His boots echoed across the scaffolding, but he stopped and turned back at the door. "I will let it go for this last festival, but if she does not see her duty done this time, then I will take care of it myself. Even if that means hailing every approaching ship and offering her to whomever is willing."

"You would not! No, Hyman, you would not."

"What I will not do is provide food and shelter to someone who will not contribute to our common good. I suggest you speak to her."

Then he was gone. Akeli crawled out of the tomato vines, brushing the wrinkles from her festival clothes and realizing far too late that the flowers had been blown from her hair when she had been out climbing in the cold wind.

"Oh, Akeli," her mother said with a weary sigh. "Come, let's go rebraid your hair."

Her mother's fingers were fast and sure, and if she lamented that there were no flowers left to replace the one's Akeli had lost she didn't say so. Instead she took out her own little box of treasures and brought out the jeweled butterfly she had never let Akeli so much as touch before.

"You know that I wore this the day I met your father," she said as she wove it into the end of Akeli's braid. "Perhaps there will be some luck in it for you. But please, Akeli, take good care of it. No going out into the wind and losing it. I would never forgive you for its loss."

Akeli nodded, pulling her braid forward over her shoulder to admire the blue and green stones set in its little silver wings. She was certain they were just colored glass, not proper jewels, but she thought it much finer than the white and pink blooms she had lost.

The clang of a landing platform from the airship meeting the end of the dock of al-Khátún echoed through the hallways and her mother caught her hand and pulled her to her feet, rushing with her to the open docking bay. The other women were already gathered around the railing there, some looking out for husbands making one of their all too infrequent visits, others just hoping to be the first to catch an unattached man's eye. Akeli pulled her hand free of her mother's grasp, preferring to linger at the back of the crowd.

The music started at once, and the women of her ship, her aunts and nieces and cousins and second cousins, took the men of the *Parjanya* by the arm and led them into the derelict zeppelin which was the heart of their ship and the only space large enough for all of them to gather together. The girders were swathed in garlands of plastic flowers. Akeli found them depressing. The light was dim enough for no one to see just how hideous they were, faded and cracked, too old to still be dragged out for every festival. But the bare girders were no atmosphere for a party either. The food at least would be delicious. All of the special treats they only had for festivals were laid out on mismatched pieces of bone china. The men of the *Parjanya* greeted the sight of all that food with even more enthusiasm than they had the sight of women.

Akeli lingered near the doorway, watching the women of her family load up plates for their guests, eating little themselves. The music was still a slow tempo, but soon it would turn rollicking and all of the women would dance. Akeli hated dancing. No, that wasn't exactly true. She loved dancing, when it was just her and her cousins. She hated dancing when strangers were there, watching. But she didn't dare try slipping away again. She knew her Uncle Hyman meant what he had said.

Someone bumped her shoulder, a latecomer rushing to join the others. He took hold of her arm, as if afraid he had nearly knocked her down. He hadn't yet noticed how solid she was.

"Sorry!" he said, letting her go then brushing both hands through his flyaway blond hair. It flopped back down on his forehead, completely unmoved by his attempts to neaten it. He took a look around the room, at the people already formed up in pairs or occasionally threes and fours. Then he looked back at Akeli with a crooked smile. She could sense the work he was doing, trying to come up with something to say. She smiled back.

"Hey," he said at last. "What food here is good? Any meat? Man, I haven't had meat in ages."

Akeli shook her head, then crossed to the nearest table, filling a plate with little samples of everything. She brought it back to him. It was all finger food, little dumplings and samosas and vegetable pies. There was no meat; the al-Khátún wasn't large enough to keep animals beyond a few reliable hens. Not like the massive floating cities she had heard crewmen from other airships tell her about. She had seen one once, far on the horizon, but villages usually kept a distrustful distance from each other.

"Thanks," he said, looking over the plate she had handed him then choosing one of the pies and stuffing the whole thing in his mouth. Unfortunately it was the last thing that had reached the table and was still hot from the oven. Akeli covered her mouth to hide her smile as he hopped on his toes, eyes streaming but still manfully chewing. "That's good," he said, although she was certain he had just burned every taste bud in his tongue. "There was some kind of spice in that; I don't know what it was but it was good. Oh, by the way," he shifted his plate to one hand and stuck the other out at her. "I'm Jason."

She took her hand down to show her smile and return his handshake. He looked at her quizzically. Then one of her cousins who was standing nearby stepped up to him, putting her hand beside her mouth to whisper in his ear. "Akeli doesn't talk," she said in a far too loud whisper. "But she's very nice otherwise." He didn't seem to notice her other hand squeezing his bicep. Akeli's smile faded away. If her cousin's means of assessing potential mates lacked subtlety, it was nothing compared to the totality of her dismissal of him among her prospects. She had turned and gone before the boy had even managed to reply, leaving him to talk to the back of her head as she sashayed to the next crewman, a burly, top-heavy fellow guaranteed to sire many strapping sons.

Akeli thought he looked dimwitted, with a touch of meanness. Not that that mattered, even if he took her cousin to wife he wouldn't be around more than a few days at a time. Still, that was as likely to pass on to his sons as his beefy biceps. Akeli preferred the nervous warmth that emanated from Jason, even if it came with a short stature and decidedly bony arms.

"That's alright then," Jason said, turning back to her after giving up on trying to speak to her cousin. "Akeli; that's a very pretty name." He flipped his hair back out of his eyes but it settled back into place almost at once.

Eating gave way to dancing far too soon for Akeli's tastes. She could see her uncle shooting glances her way. She was still standing next to Jason, but he was completely focused on his eating and not her. She suspected it was more than just meat he hadn't had in ages.

The musicians started a new song, one of Akeli's favorites. She couldn't help bouncing to the beat.

"Hey, did you want to dance? I'm not keeping you, am I?" Jason asked. One of the cousins frittered by in a blast of colored skirts and a jingle of jewelry and when she was gone his hands were quite plate-free. Akeli felt her uncle's eyes on her once more but she only shook her head and willed herself to stop bouncing. "Well, how about a tour, then? This is the first floating village I've ever visited, although I've heard tons about them. I'd love a look around, if that's OK."

Akeli nodded and threaded her arm through his, leading him out of the zeppelin, over the enclosed walkway that attached it to the next section of the ship, the fuselage of an old airliner that had been stripped and then repartitioned into living quarters. He looked around at the little touches that made one woman's door different from any others; the pictures stenciled on the metal or the plastic flowers or beads. Akeli and her mother had made an intricate mosaic out of colored paper which they had glued right to the door. It was an abstract pattern, but parts of it just suggested the shape of a vine or a flower or a butterfly.

"Is this yours?" Jason asked when she stopped to touch it. She nodded. He leaned in close to inspect it. "There must be thousands of little squares here. This must've taken days to finish." Akeli shrugged then taking his arm led him on to the first of the hydroponics rafts.

The music which was still audible down the length of the airliner was drowned out completely when she opened the door to the walkway that led from airliner to raft. Akeli caught the tail of her braid before stepping out, mindful of her mother's butterfly, then let Jason go before her through the next door.

"Wow," he said, genuinely impressed. Akeli wasn't sure why; it was just a room full of plants dangling from long racks. The sky above the glass panels was darkening, but the stars had not yet come out. It didn't look like anything. "You must have fresh food all the time, living in a place like this. I'm from space, you know. Born on a space station up in orbit. I've only been down here in atmo for a couple of months on the *Parjanya*. I suppose I look like a total rube, geeked about fresh food, but by the time any of it works its way that far up the gravity well, it's pretty limp and nasty."

Akeli looked around until she spotted a row of strawberry plants. She plucked one ripe berry and handed it to him. He bit into with undisguised pleasure. "That's good."

She led him through several more rafts of plants, occasionally pausing to let him sample this or that. He kept up a constant chatter about growing up on a space station where he was always indoors, always in the dark, and about his life now on the Parvanya in the sun and wind. Akeli was listening so attentively she didn't realize until her feet were on the open deck that she had taken him clear to the other end of the ship, to the platform under one of the four enormous balloons that kept her village afloat.

Look, Akeli. It's a parachute! I'm going to find out what's down there. I'm going to find Dad. I know that's where he went, he was always talking about it. When I find him, I'll come back for you. The three of us can live together.

Mom, too, if she wants. I'm going right now. Do you want to watch me jump, Akeli? Don't cry, sister. I'll be perfectly safe. It's a parachute! This is what it's made for. Watch me go, Akeli!

"Akeli?" She looked up at Jason's voice, almost too soft to hear over the wind. She caught her braid, remembering late again, but the butterfly was still there. She stepped back from the railing. There was nothing to see looking down anyway; nothing but the same brownish-gray clouds that covered everything. Jason leaned past her as if to see what she had been looking at.

"Ugly, isn't it? I don't care what they say, I don't think that's ever going away." He straightened and continued walking along the plat-form, around the corner to the next walkway. Akeli caught up with him in time to open the door for him.

By now the constant string of garden rooms had ceased to impress him, although he still looked around with great interest. "You know, a lot of the people up in space are talking about leaving Earth. The colonies on Mars are growing lots of food now. It doesn't do us much good, of course; it takes longer to get to the space stations than your atmo food. They've got factories there that can process it so it doesn't rot before it gets to us, but it's still largely tasteless. Actually, it's prob-ably because it's processed that it's largely tasteless." He winked at her as if looking for her to agree, but Akeli had never had food from a factory. "Lots of folks are talking about just moving to Mars. You can't go outside there, of course. No wind in your hair without bringing your own oxygen along, but they've put enough greenhouse gases in the atmo to make the temperature tolerable. Or so they say. My brother took his wife there a year ago. I'm waiting to hear from him what it's like before I make such a big move, though."

They reached the end of the line of rafts. One last plunge in and out of the wind which was growing colder as the sky grew darker and they were back in the living section of the ship. It was all workshops and storage rooms here and no one was about, but the music from the party carried faintly. Akeli tried to figure out what song it was from the beat, as she couldn't make out the melody.

"Akeli," Jason said, catching her arm before she could lead the way back to the zeppelin. "Listen, I've not done this before. I mean, I've done *that*, I've just never been to one of these floating city festivals. We have the opposite trouble back home; too many people and not enough space. Too many people moving up the well. Well, I guess that leads to your problem being opposite, with everybody leaving all the time. Someone has to stay and grow the food." She sneaked a glance up at him and saw his cheeks were just as red as she had suspected from his stammering voice. "I know it's expected, though, right?" he went on. "For the food you gave us? I mean, I ate a lot. Damn. The guys on the ship told me things, but I think they fixated on the wrong details. They assumed I knew how to get *started*."

Akeli listened, not quite looking at him. His hand was still on her arm, just above her bangles. Cheap plastic.

"I'm not sure if I'm even supposed to ask, but do you have a guy already? Like a guy on another ship or something?"

Akeli stared at the floor. He wasn't supposed to ask. At last she took his hand, dragging him behind her down the corridor away from the party, to the rooms used by the captain and those on crew duty. She took him to the narrow room with the long table and brought him to the far end, behind the big chair which was her uncle Hyman's. The wall was covered with photographs and lists of names. She didn't have to look to find Brandon's; she knew exactly where it was.

"Brandon Stone, Matarisvan. He was on the Matarisvan? Oh." It was a name of infamy. Airships were lost all the time. They would crash in storms or run into mechanical trouble far from help and disappear without a trace. Not the Matarisvan. The Matarisvan had exploded for no discernable reason shortly after leaving the village ship of Vata, in full sight of the Vata villagers and the crew of four other airships. The picture on the wall next to the list of names was taken from one of the other airships. The fire had already consumed the balloon and all that was visible were chunks of debris and little dots of crewmen plummeting to the brown clouds below.

She wondered, not for the first time, which dot was him. Or if had he been burnt to nothing in that first instant. Or if had he already fallen through the clouds by the time the man with the camera had taken the picture.

"Is that why you don't talk then? Or were you born not talking?"

Akeli just shook her head. She wasn't prepared to share everything, particularly not that.

Jason reached out and picked up the end of her braid, ostensibly to examine the little jeweled butterfly. "Akeli." She bit her lip. She thought about bringing him back to her room, but her mother wasn't so old that Uncle Hyman wouldn't expect her to do her duty as well. This was as good a place as any. He tugged gently at her braid, drawing her closer.

It wasn't like with her Brandon; it wasn't love. It wasn't exactly duty either. It was companionship, Akeli decided, and felt tears prick at the corners of her eyes. She hadn't realized how lonely she had been.

Afterwards, Jason hiked himself up on one elbow to look down at her lying on the floor of the meeting room beside him. His hair still fell over his eyes, but some of its flyaway quality had been dampened with sweat. She reached up and brushed it back, but it promptly fell back into its place. She laughed.

"Hey, you can laugh!" he said, tickling at her ribs until she squirmed. "I can hear your voice when you laugh. It's lovely." His fingers touched her ear, then traced down her neck until they found the chain she wore there. She reached up a hand to stop him then changed her mind, letting him pull the locket out of her dress.

"May I?" he asked, fingers poised at the clasp. She nodded. He opened it, leaning closer to see the picture inside. "Oh. I was expecting your fellow. Is this your baby?"

Akeli shook her head, then nodded, then shook her head again. She sat up, closing the locket and closing her hand over it.

"Was your baby?" Jason asked in a softer voice.

Akeli nodded.

"How? Well, I guess you can't tell me. Did she get sick?" She shook her head. "Accident?" Nodded. "Oh God, did she fall?" Akeli nodded again, clutching the locket tightly in her hand and willing the tears not to come. It had been such a long fall. It had seemed to take even longer for her to disappear through the clouds than it had for Kahlil with his parachute.

Jason put his hands over hers, gently opening them and then undoing the clasp on the locket so that it lay open on her palms and he could look once more at the picture within. "She looks like you, but so young. Not even two, I'd say." Akeli couldn't bring herself to nod again; she kept her face turned away. But she didn't pull the locket away from him.

"What was her name?"

She looked up at him, his eyes bright and friendly under that unruly mass of hair. His hands on hers were warm.

"Karishma."

"Karishma," Jason said, smiling at her as he closed the locket and slipped it back down the neckline of her dress. "Lovely. I wish I could have met her."

They stayed there a while longer. The feeling of companionship only grew stronger with the two of them just beside each other, not talking or touching each other or even sleeping, just being near each other and listening to the distant beat of the music.

Then the beat stopped.

"I guess it's time for me to go," Jason said with a sigh. They both got up and Jason helped her smooth out her dress and tucked the hair that had worked free from her braid behind her ears. She would have preferred to look thoroughly ravished for her uncle's benefit, but the two of them together rejoining the others at the loading area would have to be proof enough.

"The guys on the airship say sometimes we dock for days, but I guess we won't be doing that here since so few of our crew have wives in this village. But maybe we'll be back here soon. I hope." He caught her arm, pulling her to a stop in the middle of the corridor just outside the loading area. They were no longer quite alone; other couples were farewelling all around them. "Akeli. I'll write to you, but letters take so long to move from ship to ship. Please don't think I've forgotten you. I really would like to see you again."

Akeli looked down at the end of her braid twisted in her hands.

"We could marry-"

Akeli shook her head sadly, touching a hand to her belly.

"Oh right, baby first. I'd forgotten that was the rule. Well, maybe, yes?"

Akeli twisted her braid.

"Can I kiss you good-bye?"

Akeli nodded, letting go of her braid to turn her face up to his. It was worse than dancing; everyone's eyes were all over her.

Jason smiled at her, kissed her softly one more time, then turned to walk down the ramp to his airship. Akeli didn't know where to look. She didn't want to watch him go, she didn't want to see her mother or the other women of her family smiling at her, and she especially didn't want to see Uncle Hyman looking at her.

She turned and walked away from the others, away from the noise and the stuffy warmth of the room. Then she found herself walking faster, past her room, through the garden rooms, running down the length of the pods and struggling to hurry through the doors.

The *Parjanya* was nearly free when at last she reached the railing she had watched its approach from. One last line was tethering it to the village, but even as she watched the crew were casting it away.

A sudden gust of wind nearly knocked her off her feet. She caught the railing with one hand, trying to catch her spinning braid with the other. Too late, the glittering butterfly was gone, and she had not even seen it fall.

Then something slapped her in the belly and she instinctively caught it. The last mooring line, torn from some poor crewman's hands. Akeli wondered briefly what was at the other end, her village dock, or the airship?

It was like flipping a coin, wasn't it? There were worse ways of making a choice. Grasping the rope tightly, she jumped over the railing and fell.

The wind made it impossible to keep her eyes open. It drowned out her hearing, numbed her body to the sensation of anything but the rope in her hands. She was alone with her thoughts for long enough to begin to wonder whether the other end was tethered to anything at all. Her brother had landed somewhere in South America. Karishma had landed somewhere in the Indian Ocean. She tried to remember the last time she had checked the charts. What was under her now?

Then she came to the end of the rope. It nearly jerked out of her hands before she started to swing. She knew she should be climbing up, but it was all she could do to hang on.

It was very cold, in the wind.

The sound of voices shouting brought her out of her head and she opened her eyes. The airship *Parjanya* was above her, several of those beefy-armed men were working together to reel her in, and Jason was working his way down along the outrigging to meet her.

"Are you crazy?" were his first words to her once he'd nearly cracked her ribs hugging her.

"Take me with you," was all she said in return.

"Where?"

"Up. Or down. Anywhere."

"I'll get booted off this ship, you know," he told her. "Dumped at the next port. Both of us."

"Oh."

"I'm not saying no," he said, squeezing her tighter. "Just, that's what's going to happen."

"Then what?"

"Well, what do you think of Mars?"

SEAGULL AND RAVEN

Tulugaq held his hand up to the sky and counted his heartbeats. It took twelve beats for the light to move from the tip of his littlest finger to the end of his thumb.

"This is a very strange omen," the shaman said from behind him. "I don't know what it means." The two stood on the ridge overlooking the village, the blast of cold wind from over the water hitting them full in the face. Everyone else was in their stone houses, staying warm by the oil lamps and trading tales to pass the time.

What does he want me to say? Tulugaq wondered. *First he tells me the spirits say I cannot be his apprentice, then he brings me – and me alone – outside to see this. Why?*

The sun had not yet risen to mark the end of winter, but it's time was coming. The sky was already too blue for stars, but the strange moving light shone brighter than the crescent moon.

"The dead go up into the sky and become stars," Tulugaq said, thinking out loud. "But this one seems to be coming back to earth."

"I will need to speak with the spirits," the shaman said. "The spirits always know."

Yes, the spirits always know, Tulugaq thought. *But they don't always tell.*

———

Tulugaq's sister Nauja had a very distinctive smell. It wasn't like flowers. It wasn't a clean or cold smell like the ocean, and it wasn't fresh like the tundra in summer. But it was his favorite aroma. It was like being a child again, snuggling together to keep warm in their father's igloo in the winter or his tent in the summer.

The day after the slowly falling star had crossed the sky, Tulugaq was crouching patiently over a seal's air hole when the smell of his sister washed over him. It was so strong he stood and turned to greet her, but was puzzled to find he was quite alone.

It happened again the next day when he was eating with his older sister and her husband. He swore he almost felt her hands about to close over his eyes in their old childhood greeting, but behind him was nothing but the stone wall of the house.

On the third day he sensed her as he lay in the early morning halfway between sleep and waking. It was as if she lay beside him as she had every night until the day she had married. But this time he heard her voice too saying his name. He could feel her warm breath on his ear. "Tulugaq." But when he turned over, no one was there.

Tulugaq dressed and crept outside. There was a strong wind blowing over the water, pricking his face with ocean spray although he was nowhere near the water. There was an unsettled feeling to the air, as if winter had one more storm in store before the sun would come. He walked over squeaking snow to the shaman's stone house at the back of the village. There was no need to worry about waking the shaman; it was well known the man never slept.

"Something troubles you?" the shaman asked. His eyes were focused on the steady flames of his lamp, not sparing him a glance, but Tulugaq was used to this behavior. He took a seat on the hide-covered bench and told his tale with as little embellishment as he could. When he finished the shaman did not speak, only stared at the flames as if *they* had been the ones talking to him. At last he took a deep breath and sat back.

"You miss your sister, Tulugaq." It was not a question.

"Yes, but..."

"She has a husband now. And did you not tell me she was expecting a child?"

"Yes." But expecting and having were different things. She had expected other children only to have nothing to show for it. *Please, let it be a son, a child to please her husband._*Each year the winter was longer than the last and the summer shorter. There were very few girl children in Tulugaq's village. It was the same in Nauja's village.

"But you have none of these things," the shaman said.

"A husband?" The shaman shot him a look that made him squirm. "I think she needs me."

"I think this is about your need, not hers," the shaman said. Tulugaq did not know what to say to that. The shaman would not like to be argued with, but his judgment felt wrong. Now Tulugaq was the one silently focusing on the flames.

"That does not make it a lesser need," the sham said after a most uncomfortable silence. "I cannot guide you in this. You know the spirits will not speak to me of you."

Tulugaq blinked. He had not, in fact, known that. That wasn't what the shaman had told him before.

"No," the shaman said, shaking his head firmly. "I cannot be your guide."

Tulugaq went back outside, walking slowly back to his house. Not his house, really. He and Nauja had lived with their older sister and her husband after their father had died. Nauja had married and gone to live in her husband's village. There was nowhere for Tulugaq to go.

As he neared the house, a flash of motion caught the corner of his eye. A seagull was perched on top of his kayak, puffing up and flapping its wings before settling down again. It regarded him with one black bird-eye. Tulugaq touched the place where his amulet rested against his chest, under his parka. A seagull feather, given to him by his sister. Nauja. Seagull.

The bird flapped its wings again as if eager to be off then settled back down and fixed its inky stare on Tulugaq once more.

"How can I get to her? There's so much ice on the water, and it's going to storm."

But there was no point in arguing with a bird.

———

Tulugaq was well known in his Nauja's village for the singing duel in which he had bested her husband Taliriktug. That duel was still spoken of five years later, the tales told of how they had sung their insults to each other as the sun set, crept around the horizon, and then climbed the sky again. At last Taliriktug had faltered and Tulugaq had been declared the winner. Although the people of the village revered Taliriktug as their finest hunter, they admired Tulugaq's cleverness in beating their champion. He was often invited to share food with even the poorest of families in exchange for telling his version of the duel tale.

But as he paddled his kayak upstream past the first stone houses of the village, he knew something was wrong. Few people greeted him, and those who did were reluctant to meet his eyes.

Then he reached his sister's home and saw Taliriktug cleaning his own sealskin.

"Greetings, brother," Tulugaq called as he pulled his kayak up the rocky shore, far from errant waves. The seagull, still with him after three days' travel, found a perch on the roof of the stone house.

Taliriktug straightened, showing no shame for being caught doing woman's work. His eyes moved over the water behind Tulugaq, still clogged with icebergs.

"You come early this year," he said. "How was your journey?"

The urge to tell of the many times he had felt death breathing in his face these last three days was strong, but it was not the time for tales. "Treacherous. Where is my sister?"

"Your sister is gone," Taliriktug said, turning back to his work.

"Gone?"

"Since before the night of the strange light in the sky," he said, scraping away at the sealskin with the ulu. It was a useless exercise; Tulugaq could see he had already torn the skin in several places.

"Tell me, brother, what's that bird on top of your house?" Tulugaq asked.

"That's a gray bird," he said without bothering to look up.

He cannot say her name. Nauja, seagull. She's dead already. Or at least he thinks she is. He was acutely aware of his brother-in-law's reputation. Tulugaq had made him look a fool once and lived to tell the tale. He had in fact told the tale over and over again. But he knew his brother-in-law would not need much provocation before he would choose to exact a bloody retribution.

"What of the child?" he asked.

"Do you see a child here?"

It had been a girl then. Another girl. His sister's fourth. And every one of them left out in the snow.

"You are the greatest hunter of this village, I am told," Tulugaq said.

"Yes?" his sister's husband said, looking up at last from his mangled work, clutching the crescent-bladed ulu tightly.

You better than anyone could have managed to feed a girl child, even if just for the sake of my sister's heart. But such things could not be said. "You will soon find another wife," he said instead.

"Are you worried about that?" Taliriktug asked with a jaunty air that Tulugaq did not like at all. "I do not hold your family responsible. You repaid your debt to my family when I married your sister. Even if I asked you to give me another wife, how could you? Your mother is dead, and you do not have a wife."

Tulugaq's hands curled into fists, but he held his tongue. His brother-in-law was deliberately provoking him. They both knew the story well. His father had owed a debt to Taliriktug's father, one that he had sworn to repay by raising a daughter to be the future wife of the other man's son. This would be an easy debt to repay, as his mother had had many girl children already. Girls - all but one left in the snow - and no boys. But when Nauja was born, Tulugaq had come too. His parents had tried to raise them both, for Nauja was already promised to another, and Tulugaq was the son they had longed for. Tulugaq knew his mother had fed her husband and babies first, and only then did she eat. His father, like Tulugaq himself, had been a poor hunter. She had slowly and silently starved to death by the time Tulugaq was five.

Taliriktug was watching his face closely. "If you wish, we could go out hunting for your sister. You and I."

Tulugaq tasted blood in his mouth and realized he had bitten through his tongue. Two men go hunting and only one returns. It happened all the time. As their eyes met, neither of them had any doubt as to which would return.

"No," he said. "I wish nothing from you." He got back in his kayak but paddled up the river rather than back out to sea, slipping between floes of ice. The seagull swept past his head, leading the way further upstream.

He had felt his sister near him again just last night, whispering his name. Why would she call to him if she were already dead?

He thought of the strange light he had seen in the sky, but that had been coming back from the sky, not going up into it. It couldn't have been his sister.

Or had she gone up then fallen back down again?

Tulugaq shook his head to clear it. He followed the seagull up the river until it was too clogged with ice to continue. He left his kayak wedged behind some mossy boulders, protecting it as much as he could from wind and water. He had no wife to make him another if this one was swept away. He took his harpoon out of the kayak. He was already growing hungry. He did not want to spare the time to fish now, but perhaps some animal would happen to cross his path as he walked. He did not think he could bring himself to kill a bird just at the moment.

The seagull had waited patiently until he emerged from behind the rocks then resumed its guiding flight, north over the open tundra.

He trudged over the snow for hours. The short almost-day faded back to total night and it grew harder to keep his eye on the bird above him. At last his guide spiraled down to disappear behind a rise in the tundra, too slight to be called a hill. Tulugaq, weary as he was from the long walk after three days of kayaking, broke into a run to see where the seagull had disappeared to.

Beyond the rise was a single stone house. It wasn't unusual to find stone houses built on the tundra, the caribou came here to graze in the summer months, but there was only the one structure, and it was not large enough to be a common house. Tulugaq clutched his harpoon tightly as he advanced. He could see the seagull now, preening on the roof. The house was old. Some of the stones had started to tumble down. But if there had been others he could see no sign of them now in the darkness, not so much as an outline of stones on the tundra.

Then he heard it: the sharp squall of a baby.

Tulugaq crouched low and crawled through the narrow opening into the house. Someone – a woman – was standing over a blubber oil stove, her back to him as she cooked strips of meat. The crying was coming from a large pile of caribou hides on the opposite side of the bench from the stove.

As he straightened, the woman turned and he released a breath he hadn't even known he was holding. It was Nauja! She looked the worse for her ordeal. Patches of her skin were gray with frostbite, and there was a dead look in her eyes. But she was alive.

"Nauja!" he cried, leaning his harpoon against the wall so he could have both hands free to embrace her. "Sister, I thought you were dead."

"Dead?" she repeated. "No. Not dead. Not yet."

"And this is my niece?" he asked, extracting the infant from the tangle of furs. As he held her, she stopped crying but continued to make snuffling complaining sounds.

"What is her name?" he asked.

"I don't know," his sister said and turned back to the cooking meat.

"Taliriktug thinks you are dead," he said. "Are you going to go back to him?"

"No. If I am dead to him now, I shall remain so."

Tulugaq's chest felt too tight for his heart. His sister had been sunshine itself as a child, effortlessly cheering her brother and father after the loss of her mother. She had been radiant at her marriage to Taliriktug, openly pleased to be matched with such a famous hunter.

But every year since when Tulugaq had paddled his kayak up the coast to visit her a little more light had gone out of her. Like her mother, she seemed cursed to have only girl children.

And yet she had one now, a living breathing child, and she would not even look at it.

"You should come home with me," Tulugaq said. "There are many hunters without wives. Many of them still ask me about you. You broke so many hearts when you married Taliriktug! It would take no time at all to find you a new husband, even if it meant taking on your child as well."

Nauja seemed not to have heard him. The baby was complaining more loudly now, rooting against his parka in the search of something he did not have.

"The shaman said something strange to me before I left. Do you remember last summer, when I told you he told me that the spirits said he could not teach me? I'm sure that's what he said. But just before I left he said that the spirits will not speak to him about me at all. What do you think that means?"

Nauja did not reply. She took a small bite from one of the strips of meat, made a face, and resumed cooking.

"Where did you get the meat?" he asked.

"It as here in the house when I got here," she said.

"Someone must live here."

"No one lives here."

"I suppose it's a summer house. What kind of meat is that? Caribou? Are you sure it's any good?"

But she had lapsed back into silence. He looked down at the squirming baby. Her moans were getting louder now and she would be crying again at any moment. He rocked her in his arms, clucking his tongue at her. She quieted a little.

"Maybe we shouldn't go back to the village. I mean, it's up to you where we go, but I think what the shaman was saying…"

"Put the baby down," Nauja interrupted.

"I think she's hungry," Tulugaq said but did as his sister asked. It was quite warm in the stone house; he did not understand the need for all the furs. The baby wailed, thrashing about in the jerky movements of the newly born, not happy to be laid down and ignored again.

Then the smell of his sister washed over him again. Not coming from behind him, as this time it should have. It wasn't coming from the baby either, although that was closer.

Tulugaq dropped to his knees to peer under the stone slab of the bench. Scattered beneath the bench were bones, picked clean of meat and broken so that someone could suck out the marrow. He stared straight into the empty sockets of a human skull. And the smell of his sister was so strong it made his eyes sting. He picked up the splintered half of a thigh bone and held it in his hand.

"Nauja?"

His words were choked off by fingers like talons biting into his throat. His sister seemed suddenly taller, towering over him as she squeezed the air out of him. Then he realized that was only because he had fallen to his knees. He clawed at her hands, trying to break her grip, and was horrified when the skin tore away from her flesh in tattered strips.

Not Nauja. A witch has taken her skin. Just like in the stories. Spirits help me; a witch has taken my sister's skin!

"N…"

But speaking was impossible, and judging by the dark fury in her eyes quite useless. His eyes darted about and found where he had left his harpoon on the other side of the room. Completely out of reach.

Stars exploded before his eyes, brighter than the false comet against the increasingly blackening room. The room was turning black and sliding away from him when he realized he still held his sister's broken thigh bone in his hand. With all the strength he could muster in his rapidly dying body he thrust it up into the witch's heart.

She hissed and spun away and Tulugaq fell forward on his hands, sucking in great gulps of air. The room spun, went motionless, then spun the other way. He got to his feet and lurched across the floor to his harpoon. He turned back to see the witch in Nauja's skin crawling toward the screaming baby, the thigh bone still protruding from her bleeding chest. He gave a great cry, more of frustration and grief than war cry, and charged with his harpoon, driving it through her body.

She looked up at him, her big eyes pleading. And yet there was nothing behind those eyes. How could he have thought this was his sister? At last she fell limp against him and he shoved her away, harpoon and all. The body slumped against the wall, hands still clutching the bone in her chest. Hands with skin hanging off in tatters.

But there was no red flesh beneath, no glimpse of meat or tendon that he had ever seen. Beneath she was a sickly green, smooth as sealskin.

Tulugaq collapsed on the bench. He clenched his head in his hands, tearing fiercely at his hair, and wept as he had never wept in his life. Not even as a child when his mother had died.

His sister was gone.

His sister, who had a place in the world, was gone. And he, who had none, remained.

After a while his sobs quieted and he became aware of the other being crying in the stone house. His niece. Wiping his eyes, he once more untangled her from the caribou hides and picked her up. This time she did not cease her cries.

"Hush, baby girl," he said, rocking her in his arms, but she would have none of it. "You need a name. Is that why you cry so? You have no name?" He sorted through the pile of hides with one hand, choosing the softest to wrap her in, but carefully this time, tucking her flailing limbs close to her body. Then, stopping only to pull his harpoon from the remains of the witch, he went back outside.

The air was cool after the close heat of the stone house. He found it soothing, but his niece was not soothed. He examined the walls of the stone house carefully then, using his harpoon for leverage, sent the whole thing collapsing down, as much of a cairn for his sister as he was able to make.

The seagull had gone. How could he find his way back across the tundra without his guide?

"Nauja!" he called, hoping the bird was somewhere nearby, close enough to hear his call.

The babe in his arms quieted. He looked down in surprise. She looked back up at him with dark eyes of merry intelligence, so like his sister's.

"Is that your name? Are you Nauja?" Her only answer was to close her eyes and fall asleep.

There was a rustle of feathers atop the ruins of the stone house, but the loud caw was not the call of a seagull. This time it was a raven, his own namesake, come to guide him.

"Are you guiding me home?" he asked. The bird did not acknowledge him, busy as he was picking nits out of his feathers. "But it won't be home, will it? Or at least not the home I knew. Very well, lead on then. Nauja and I will follow."

After all, there was no point in arguing with a bird.

MOTHER RIVER

"Where is he, where is he?"

Mara's constantly repeated question irritated Prithvi. They were meant to cover all the men of the People, not just each their own beloved. But Prithvi held her tongue. She knew the real source of her foul mood was the long day of being heavily pregnant under a hot sun, up on the mud brick wall where the dusty wind could easily find her and scour her sweaty skin with grit. The last hour with the setting sun in their eyes had been particularly tortuous. But she also knew that while the murmuring was a distraction to her, it slowed Mara down not at all. She fired arrow after arrow with scarcely a pause between, and she very rarely missed.

"I see him," Prithvi said, and turned to fire her next arrow to their left, well outside of the area they were meant to be covering and nearly out of her own range. Mara fired her own after it, and the nomad that was their target fell from his horse, giving their husband Mrugesh a little more breathing space.

"He'll be fine," Prithvi said, returning her attention to the more immediate battle. "Daksha is with him."

"There are more enemies than yesterday," Mara said.

"Yes, but they're falling back all the same." The nomads had turned about and were falling back to their encampment on the banks of the river. The low hills hid the camp and water both from view. Prithvi didn't know if her grandmother's stories were true, that once the Sarsuti River had flowed right up to the city walls and had spread just as far beyond the other bank, but she could remember being able to see the river from the tops of the walls when she was a girl. Now Sarsuti hunkered down low and out of sight, and the nomads hunkered down with her.

They weren't retreating, they were just breaking off for dinner and sleep, scarcely bothering to cover their withdrawal. They knew the People were too few to pursue them.

The sun had still been high in the sky when the nomads had started their attack. Now the stars were starting to come out and Prithvi's arms were shaky from all the aiming and firing. The dull ache in her low back that had been plaguing her all day was growing more pronounced as well. She closed her eyes, so weary she would gladly sleep on the wall rather than make the walk back to their house in the center of the city.

"Mrugesh!" Mara cried, and Prithvi brought her bow back up, turning to bear on the last place she had seen him. He had spurred his horse on, chasing down the departing nomads. Prithvi couldn't pick his voice out of the roar of sound below her, but she could see her brother Daksha's face as he yelled her husband's name, calling him back.

Too late. Two of the nomads wheeled their mounts around, cutting off Mrugesh's retreat. Then they came at him, swords raised high. Mara and Prithvi both took aim and fired. Prithvi was certain it was useless; they had never tried to hit a target so far away before. But she couldn't celebrate when both arrows hit their mark; they had both aimed for the same attacker, and as he fell, disappearing in the dust of the battlefield, the other brought his sword down on Mrugesh's skull.

"No!" Mara said, and Prithvi dropped her bow to catch her before she fainted.

"Help me!" she called out, trying to ease Mara to the ground without crushing little Diti still sleeping in the sling across Mara's back. Two of the other women rushed forward to hold Mara long enough for Prithvi to get Diti free. The girl didn't even wake. She was curled up in a sweaty little ball, fist to mouth, softly snoring. Her face scrunched up at the jostling but she curled against Prithvi's shoulder and resumed her snoring without ever quite waking.

"I can walk," Mara said, although she looked wan.

Prithvi headed down the steep staircase, forced to take them slowly despite the urgency. The ache in her back twinged at each step down and it was a relief to reach the ground below. Mara came down after, the bangles tied to the cord around her waist jingling at each step. She untied them as they hurried down the dark streets, slipping half over one hand and half over the other before reaching for Diti. Prithvi didn't bother putting her own bangles back on. She doubted Mrugesh would notice, although her grandmother surely would.

"Prithvi, what if he dies? What will become of us without him?" Mara whispered. There had been few enough men left among the People before the nomads had surrounded the city. There were even fewer now.

"Daksha will take us in," Prithvi said. "Both of us." She was whispering too. Not that she was afraid of being overheard, it was just that everything echoed so loudly in the empty parts of the city. Especially on nights like this one, when the air was still and thick with heat.

Mrugesh had been laid out in the main hall of their house near the fire pit. Mara rushed at once to his side, clasping his hand to her chest and sobbing his name. Prithvi hung back. Her husband wasn't a bad man, but in nearly two years of marriage he had never ceased to be a stranger to her. She watched as Mara fussed over him, but he scarcely responded. A moan, a flutter of eyelids. The two healer women were pressing cloth after cloth to his wound but the blood kept coming.

Prithvi turned away, slipping through the kitchen and across the courtyard until she reached the house sanctum. There she knelt before the statue of Sarsuti: their river, their goddess, their mother. It was quiet here and dark; the two oil lamps that burned to either side of Sarsuti cast more shadows than light, it seemed. Prithvi ran her hands over her swollen belly then wrapped her arms around it, hugging the child within her as she bent forward to press her forehead to the cool stone of the statue's feet.

She had come here once before, asked a boon of her goddess, and gotten it. It had been a blasphemy; she was not even a novitiate let alone the high priestess. The feeling of it still haunted her, to be herself and yet not, to have this immense alien thing within her, not controlling her precisely, although she had done nothing but what it had wanted her to do. And she knew that she had not yet begun to pay the price for that magic, although she would, soon.

She would never do it again for herself. But should she for the sake of the People? Although no one was caught saying it, everyone seemed to be hearing it all over the city; the People thought the goddess had abandoned them. Prithvi alone knew she was still there. Did that give her an obligation? She bit her lip, pressing her forehead harder against the stone feet of her goddess. She wished she knew what to do.

"Why are you here and not with your husband?"

Prithvi sat back on her heels, wiping at her cheeks although the only moisture there was sweat, not tears. "I came here to pray."

Anuradha, high priestess of Sarsuti, was mother of all the People in the rituals, but was also Prithvi's grandmother in the more mundane sense. Since the death of her husband she had taken over the role of chieftain as well, and none had questioned her right to do so. No one would dare.

"Praying for Mrugesh?"

"Yes," Prithvi said, but her voice caught.

"Liar," Anuradha said, not angrily. She had to lean on Prithvi's shoulder for support to get down, but she had soon settled herself comfortably and lifted her hands in prayerful salute and Prithvi did the same. "You pray for your child."

"Is that wrong?"

"To pray for a healthy child who will grow to take her place among the People, no," Anuradha said. "But that isn't what you pray for, is it?"

"No," Prithvi admitted. "I pray to the mother goddess to lift her curse on the People and bless me with a son." She kept her eyes away from her grandmother's. Pray was not the word for what she had done.

"Vanity," Anuradha said, but then sighed. "I don't blame you. To give your husband a son and an heir, one he could look upon this night before he passes on, would be a tremendous gift. But Sarsuti remains far from us. She seldom speaks, even to me. Her anger has not yet lifted."

"I just want a son, a fine warrior like..." She had nearly said "like his father", but Anuradha had a way of making her stumble over even half-lies. "Like Daksha," she said instead, because that was true too.

"Vanity," Anuradha said again. Prithvi kept her gaze studiously on Sarsuti, although she could feel her grandmother watching her intently. She should not have said she just wanted a son; it was as much as admitting he wouldn't be an heir. Not for the first time in the last nine months, she suspected her grandmother already knew everything but was waiting for Prithvi to confess.

The heat and the smell of incense were making her head swimmy; for an instant the flickering of the oil lamps had make it seem that Sarsuti had blinked at her, a slow, comforting gesture. Prithvi looked over at her grandmother gazing on the same statue, but if she had seen the blink she did not react. Maybe it wasn't the People the goddess had abandoned; maybe it was just her high priestess.

"Come, let's go see to your husband," Anuradha said, grunting her way back onto her old feet but then stooping to help Prithvi up. Mara was still at Mrugesh's side, nursing Diti without relinquishing his hand. Prithvi knelt on his other side, looking down on his ashen face. His eyes were not quite closed, and she could see him watching her through the narrow slits. He didn't try to speak or even to open his eyes all the way, just kept watching her.

"Prithvi."

Prithvi turned at the sound of her brother's voice, getting to her feet so she could bury herself in his chest, feel his arms around her.

"He fought well," Daksha said. "Those nomads paid dearly for his life."

"They're too numerous," Prithvi said. "They can afford to pay dearly for each life within these walls and still have men to spare."

"I need you to see something. Can Mara spare you?"

"Yes. There's not really anything for me to do here, anyway."

"Come, then, let's make you useful." Daksha led her out of the house, through the streets where the People still lived and the smell of bread hot off the pan filled the air, then through the streets where there were no more People to the city wall. They were on the opposite end of the city than her watch station, looking downriver rather than upriver.

"They are closer here," Prithvi said. The lights from campfires scattered near the river bluffs looked like dim but warm stars.

"Yes. I'm thinking we should station you and Mara here for a few nights. The other women don't have your range."

"The tents aren't that close."

"No, but sometimes one or two wander out of the camp and gets close enough where you could give them a firm warning."

"Is this what you wanted me to see?"

"No. Look at this," he placed a knife on her hand. She brought it close to her eyes to examine it in the flickering torchlight.

"What is this?" she asked, rubbing at the blade.

"Iron."

"Are you sure?" She had heard of iron from the traders who still passed through the city. None of them had ever actually had iron objects with them, but they claimed the cities to the north were using it for all their weapons while the People were forced to melt down and reuse what bronze they had left now that the tin supply had disappeared.

"They all have it. Their swords and knives are made of it, their arrows are tipped with it. What else could it be?"

"This doesn't give them as much of an advantage as their numbers do," Prithvi said.

"You're right. But I think they're building something as well."

"Building what?"

"Something to bring down our walls, I fear."

Prithvi bit her lip. The People had always been peace-loving, as their mother Sarsuti had bid them to be. The walls around their city were there only to control trade, to allow the city officials to tax the traders as they came in through the wide open gateways. Now the gateways were sealed with hastily constructed doors to keep the nomadic raiders out, but the walls were not stone like the cities of the north, they were mud bricks.

"What can we do?" Prithvi asked. "Perhaps the time has come to just open our doors. Once inside the city they will see we have nothing left worth conquering and they'll go."

"They would certainly go, but I doubt very much they'd leave any one of us alive. I have seen them up close; these are men who have been too hungry for too long. Our Mother has been hard on the People, but she has been harder still on her other children. The nomad's clothes are not familiar to me. They've come a long way, drawn by tales of a city filled with gold. They'll probably blame us for the spread of those lies."

"Or kill us for keeping secret the location of all that gold," Prithvi sighed. Her back twinged again and she pressed the heel of her hand on it. She felt achy all over and desperately wanted to sleep.

"No, we can't try surrendering now," Daksha said. "I'll have to ride out at dawn, charge their camp and try to destroy whatever it is they're building just over those hills."

"They will just start over again," Prithvi said.

"And I will destroy it again. What else is there to do?"

Prithvi had no answer for that. "You'd think they'd notice," she said at last. "That so few men ride out, but the walls are covered with archers."

"Maybe they have. Maybe that's why they're still fighting to get in. A city full of women is a treasure in its own right." He looked at her, his face smiling but his eyes serious and watchful, just like their grandmother's. "Maybe that's why you want to open the gates, eh? You want to be a nomad's woman?"

"If that were true I would have walked out months ago," Prithvi said. "I'm still here."

"A good thing, too," Daksha said, hugging her once more and placing a kiss on the top of her head. "When I'm chieftain I'm going to need your council even more than I do now."

"No, you need me here to listen while you council yourself. When do I ever say anything?"

"You don't have to. It's all in your eyes, little sister."

"What's in my eyes now?"

Daksha bent down to look into her kohl-rimmed eyes, fingers pressing lightly on her earlobes to keep her still. "You're thinking that in the morning we should leave the routine watch on the upriver side of the city but place all the other archers downriver, with those with the longest range positioned nearest the enemy camp." He peered closer. "With pitch? I agree. Excellent plan."

Prithvi laughed, perhaps too hard as her abdomen jostled and then clenched hard. She rubbed her hands over her belly until it loosened once more.

"I should take you back to Mrugesh now," Daksha said. "But be sure you sleep as much as you can. I'll need you in the morning. It gives me courage, knowing you are watching over me when I fight."

"I will always be there," Prithvi promised. "Mara and I both."

"Yes, Mara," Daksha said with a sly look that said he knew exactly what she was laying the groundwork for. "I'll need Mara as well. She is your sister, as you are mine."

Prithvi expected to return to find Mrugesh gone, but he was still breathing, no better but no worse than before. Mara had laid down beside him, Diti snuggled between them just as she always slept between Prithvi and Mara.

Prithvi knelt at Mrugesh's side and pressed his hand between hers. His eyes were as before, watching her intently through the narrowest of slits. Prithvi leaned down to press a kiss to the side of his forehead that wasn't still oozing blood. "I'm sorry," she said. She wasn't sure she was, she wasn't even sure she had anything to be sorry for, but she felt she ought to say it. If he really was watching her from under those eyelids he didn't seem to hear her.

Prithvi lay down beside him on the stone floor of the hall and closed her eyes, but exhausted as she was sleep would not come. Instead of dreams she was awash in memories.

———

Mara had already been married to Mrugesh for two years when Prithvi joined their family. Mara adored their husband to a degree Prithvi simply could not grasp. Again and again she'd ask what it was about him that made him so special in Mara's eyes. Every detail that Mara would list, and there were many, Prithvi could appreciate too, but not like Mara did. Mrugesh was indeed fine-looking, well-respected, kind, and had a voice of a pleasing timbre. There was no reason Prithvi didn't feel as Mara did, no fault to point out as the cause of her lack of feeling. Clearly the fault was in her. There was a coldness in her heart and nothing would ever warm it.

Or so she had thought. Then she had met Kochai.

Kochai had been traveling with a caravan of traders, although he wasn't a trader himself but a shepherd from the high mountain villages returning from a journey to the ocean cities. Mrugesh had done good business with that caravan, buying gold ingots and gemstones and selling all of the pieces of finished jewelry he had on hand. As was his custom he had invited the traders to stay in his home, and because he valued hospitality above all things he extended his invitation even to those he had had no business with, including Kochai, who was only traveling with the caravan because the roads were dangerous for a man alone.

Mara had been heavily pregnant at the time, easily tired and prone to illness; she had stayed in their bedchamber the entire time the traders were there. So it fell to Prithvi to play the wife, serving the food and seeing to her husband's guests. Mrugesh had later praised how attentive she was, but in truth from the moment Kochai stepped into the room no one existed but him.

He wasn't like the men of the People. He was short but heavily muscled where the men of the People were tall and wiry; his hair was short and curly where the People always wore theirs long and straight. Nor did he look like the traders, for they were all ocean people. From the way his eyes followed her around the room she guessed she was as exotic to him as he was to her.

"What does this mean?" he asked - much later after the dinner had been consumed and the traders and Mrugesh were too far into their drinking and storytelling to notice the two of them slip away — touching his fingers to the vermilion in the part of her hair.

"Among the People, it means I'm married," she told him.

"I thought these bangles meant you were married?" Hooking his finger through the hoops around her wrist then letting them fall one at a time.

"The gold ones do."

"And the necklace?" Gently lifting the pendant that hung between her breasts.

"That too."

"And the rings in your ears?" Touching more ear lobe than jewelry now.

"Those are just pretty."

His laugh, something warm spread through her belly at his laugh and she at last knew what Mara had been trying to tell her for more than a year.

They had been in the shadows of the courtyard, far from the fire pit in the main hall, but when Kochai tilted his head to look at her the gold ring in his ear glinted. Prithvi sought out the source of this new light; a lamp in the sanctum was still burning. Mara must have said extra prayers before going to bed and had left the lamp at the statue's base. The oil was nearly gone and the flame was beginning to founder. Sarsuti seemed to dance in the flickering light.

The dance of creation, Prithvi thought, remembering the story. She will create her own lover to sire her most favored children.

"Please, goddess," Prithvi murmured as Kochai nuzzled closer to her neck. "Please lift your curse."

As the last of the oil burned away and the flame died, Prithvi saw Sarsuti cease dancing, lowering her arms then, quite distinctly, nodding her head.

And in the sudden darkness there was just her and Kochai, and that warm feeling began to spread. She closed her eyes as his mouth found hers, but something within her was opening its eyes. Something, no someone huge was suddenly there in her mind, filling her. She wasn't big enough to contain it. She gasped aloud at the feel of it. Then it flowed further, beyond her mind into her body, and her arms were moving, wrapping around Kochai, and Prithvi let it happen.

———

Mara shook her awake in the gray before dawn.

"Mrugesh?" Prithvi asked sleepily.

"He still breathes," she said, "but I don't think he's aware. He looks and looks but I don't think he sees me."

"I'm sorry, Mara."

Mara just nodded, and Prithvi recognized all the signs of Mara working hard not to cry. "Daksha wants us on the wall now."

"If you want to stay..."

"No," Mara said, swallowing hard. "My place is there. The healers who are tending to Mrugesh are going to watch over Diti so she can stay here. So he won't be alone." She stood, then bent to help Prithvi up. Prithvi got to her feet but before she had completely straightened her belly clenched down hard.

"What is it? Is it..."

"No," Prithvi said. "It's just from sleeping on the stone floor, I think. I'm fine now."

Mara looked skeptical. She fussed about Prithvi, then Diti, then Mrugesh, and Prithvi knew she was waiting to see if it would happen again, to see if Prithvi was about to go into labor. But Prithvi truly was fine, and the city around them had grown quiet with everyone else either preparing to ride out or taking their places on the wall.

"Come on, then," Mara said at last, and the two of them jogged as fast as Prithvi could manage. Someone had brought their bows to the downriver wall, probably at Daksha's order. Prithvi took up an arrow soaked in pitch and moved closer to the nearest torch, picking out her first target.

The sound of a horn carried through the still morning air. Prithvi wondered why her brother would blow a horn to announce a charge that was meant to come as a surprise, then realized it wasn't coming from the gate at all. It was coming from the far wall.

"They're attacking us!" Prithvi cried, suddenly wishing she was at her usual post.

"There go the men," Mara said. But they turned upriver out of the gate, abandoning Daksha's plan in order to defend the far side of the city.

"Do you feel that wind?" Prithvi said.

"It's like it's blowing out of an oven," Mara said.

"Not just hot," Prithvi said. "It's blowing hard. It's blowing downriver."

"So?"

"So we can't hit their camp from here, but if we use the pitch arrows to create a wall of fire..."

"...the wind would drive it into their camp..."

"...trapping them against the river. At the very least they won't be able to come to the aid of their men upriver."

"What if the wind changes?"

"The walls will protect us. We could retreat to the center of the city if we have to."

Mara sent the younger cousins scurrying up and down the wall to deliver this plan to the other women. When Prithvi fired her first arrow it was quickly followed by dozens more. The dry, late autumn grass caught easily and soon everything downriver was lost in the smoke.

"Send word for the normal watches to remain; the rest of us are going over to the upriver wall to help in the battle," Prithvi said. Once more they were jogging across the city, the jingle of bangles tied to the women's waists sounding almost merry. But Prithvi couldn't keep up.

"What's the matter?" Mara asked, having had to turn back to find her. "Is it the baby?"

"I don't think so," Prithvi said. "It's not painful like when you had Diti. Just an ache, really."

"I think you should go back home," Mara said.

"No, I'll be there. But go on, I can't run."

"Are you sure?"

"Yes. Daksha needs you. Watch over him?"

"I will," Mara said, giving her a tight hug.

"I'll be along," Prithvi promised. The ache relented somewhat so long as she kept walking, and there would be water jars at the wall. Her mouth was sticky with thirst.

When she finally reached the wall all thoughts of water flew from her mind, and she deeply wished she had found the strength to run. The women were drawing and firing, drawing and firing, but the grassy plain below was filled with men. It was a sea of brown leather and gray wool only occasionally broken by the brightly dyed cotton of the city dwellers. For each tall, long-haired, bare-chested man of the People there were a dozen or more nomads surrounding him, cutting him off from the others, cutting him down. Prithvi's eyes searched and searched, but there was no sign of Daksha.

"We burned an empty camp," she murmured to herself. Then she lost all thoughts but those needed to aim and fire. Her thirst was easy to ignore, the growing pressure below her belly was not. But she remembered Mara's labor, the pain she could scarcely breathe through. This was not that; she still had time.

The sun had climbed halfway to noon when Mara appeared at her side. "We're running out of arrows!"

"Sound the horn," Prithvi said. "Daksha will have to bring them back inside and try to defend from the gates. We..." But the end of her thought was lost as she tried to take a step and felt a rush of strangeness move through her.

"Prithvi?"

"Here he comes," Prithvi said, clutching Mara's hand and squatting low against the wall.

"Who, Daksha?" But the sudden paleness to Mara's face meant that Prithvi didn't have to answer. "Why didn't you say something?"

"I didn't know," Prithvi said.

"We have to get you home."

"No time."

"At least off the wall. Prithvi!"

"It'll have to be here."

The women around them, long since out of arrows, quickly moved to deal with this new emergency. Someone gave her a cloth soaked in cool well water, someone else brought a blanket from one of the houses closest to the wall to spread beneath her. Prithvi wasn't really aware of any of it, aside from a momentary annoyance when some well-meaning soul untied the bangles from her waist and pushed them onto her wrists. A child born to an unbangled mother would be terribly unlucky. Prithvi fought back a harsh laugh.

It was all over in a matter of minutes. Prithvi was too exhausted to protest when many hands lifted her, carried her down off the wall, and settled her on what she belatedly recognized as her grandmother's ceremonial palanquin, her baby snuggled up against her. She drifted in and out of sleep, the rocking of the palanquin hypnotic and the air inside hot and close. It was only when they reached her house and set her back down on the ground that she looked at the baby in her arms.

A son. And under the blood and wetness his hair was a cap of tight, dark curls.

Prithvi drifted off to sleep again but woke in a sudden panic. She was in her bedchamber, little Diti napping beside her. Prithvi could swear someone had just spoken her name, some woman, but no one else was in the room.

Where was her son?

Prithvi got to her feet, tossing aside the cloths someone had pressed against her. She wasn't bleeding anymore, but her legs were shaky and she had to reach out for support, finding herself clinging to the wall until the weakness passed. She slowly made her way down the stairs.

There was still the distant sound of battle, but the house was silent. More than silent, it was if it were muffled by the hot, still air. The wind from the morning had died down and the sky above was a cloudless blue, but the air was a nightmare of sweltering heat. Prithvi, making her careful way down the steep staircase, was soon soaked in a sweat that gave her no relief. The air was too moist for the sweat on her skin to dry and cool her.

"Am I ill?" she murmured to herself. "Is that why they took my son?"

Then she heard a soft sound coming from the sanctum. She hurried down the last few steps but kept her shoulder to the wall to circle the courtyard. She wasn't ready to try walking on her own yet.

As she reached the sanctum she saw that someone had taken down the statue of Sarsuti, replacing it with another, more fearsome image. She knew what the statue depicted, she had seen this aspect before painted on the walls of the bath house, the walls that told the story of the People. This was Sarsuti in her dark mother aspect; not the nurturing, soft mother with breasts overflowing with milk, but the mother who would toss you into the middle of the raging river to teach you to swim, the mother with swords to cut away any hindrances.

And at the feet of this dark mother was Anuradha, singing and making intricate gestures with her hands. And on the ground between them was Prithvi's son. He was still covered in birth blood and was flailing spastically, his little face quite purple, but no sound coming from his throat.

Prithvi tried to rush to him but Anuradha, never turning her head, cast one of her hand gestures over her shoulder and Prithvi felt her knees buckle. She fell to the paving stones, gasping and fighting the wave of blackness that was trying to wash over her.

"Prithvi."

That voice again, the one that had woken her. Whose was it? It sounded so familiar.

"Mother?" she asked, or tried to. Like her son, something had taken her voice.

"Yes, I am Mother. As are you. As is she, in her way." Prithvi, with great effort, lifted her head. She could see her grandmother, gesturing and singing still, but there was no one else there.

"Help me."

"Only as the left hand helps the right hand, for we are as one. I do not speak, do not expect to be listened to. I act and you act, together. You are I. Remember. Now stand."

And Prithvi found she was standing, and more she was knocking her grandmother aside and taking up her son. He was still and silent, and when Prithvi touched his face his head moved in a way no baby's head should move. Prithvi touched him again. This had been no natural newborn death, and no magical one either. While she had been pinned to the ground conversing with her goddess, her grandmother had snapped his tiny neck. Prithvi was shocked beyond grief, beyond anger. She could feel both distantly, but drawing closer.

Anuradha got to her feet. She was tearful and distressed. Prithvi almost felt pity. If only she hadn't seen that look of triumph that had flitted across her grandmother's face just before she had gotten up.

"I prayed for him, but it was already too late," Anuradha said. Prithvi didn't listen, just clutched the little body tight. "It's the curse, Prithvi. Sarsuti has taken back every male child of the People for years now. I'm sorry."

"But," said Prithvi, touching her son's tiny head, the curls gone hard and spiky as the blood had dried, "he wasn't one of the People."

"He was; he was your son. Did you really think it would matter who the father was to Sarsuti? Sarsuti was consort to the sky, and their children were the people of the mountains. Sarsuti was consort to the sea, and their children were the people of the sea. But Sarsuti came to the center of things, was consort to herself alone, and gave birth to the People."

"I know it," Prithvi said. "How well do I know it. She told me the tale herself, once. I thought maybe it was a dream, but I knew it wasn't. She came to me the night this one was conceived." She felt odd, as if she had drunk some strange wine that had filled her with bravado but left her head clear. She felt strong. "Mrugesh entertains many visitors, and I've talked with them all. I've spoken to the traders who come from the sea, and Sarsuti even there is fading. Their ships cannot sail up her waters without running aground when once she was as deep as the sea itself. And I've spoken with men from the mountains, and the innumerable streams which were once her hair have changed. Some have disappeared, but some are flowing the other way, to other rivers."

"This is known to all of us," Anuradha said. "Where else did you think our farmers had gone when they abandoned us but to other rivers?"

"And yet only we, the People, are cursed. Sarsuti is mother to us all, why only are we punished this way?" Prithvi held her son tighter then spoke the words that had been whispering inside of her for years. "Why only since your husband died have we been cursed?"

Anuradha moved with the speed of a striking cobra, slapping Prithvi hard across her face. "My husband was the first of our losses, and no number of losses since will ever match my grief for that first."

"That," Prithvi said, touching her hot cheek, "is not a denial."

Anuradha raised her hand again, looking even more fearsome than the statue towering before her, but she lowered it again, rage crumbling into grief. "What does it matter? We've lost all. Don't you hear it?"

Prithvi realized at that moment that she was hearing something, had in fact been hearing it for some time. "The walls," she said, trying to picture what the nomads could possibly have built that could make such noises.

"It's all over. All I've done for naught," Anuradha said.

"You thought to be dark mother for all of us," Prithvi said.

"Yes." A dreamy look was on Anuradha's face, but not one of pleasant dreams.

"Cut away our hindrances?"

Anuradha's focus came back to the moment. "You don't understand; they were going to leave."

"Who?"

"The men. They were going to follow the farmers, go to other cities on the other river, try to find a place for ourselves among some other people."

"How did you think we were going to survive with only women?" Prithvi said. "Already those of my age are married to men far older, many wives to a husband. What of Diti and her generation? Who will they marry?"

"We are the People. We were born of Sarsuti alone. We will know she has forgiven us when we too give birth alone."

"Forgiven us? She was never punishing us. It's been you, all this time."

"No, not me," Anuradha said. She suddenly looked very old and confused. "Sarsuti lives in the hearts of all mothers, but mine more than any other. It was her. I did her bidding. Everything she has asked, I have done."

"You lie. She has spoken to me." Prithvi could feel the strength in her growing, even as the drunken sense of fearlessness grew. Wasn't this Sarsuti? It certainly wasn't Prithvi's own heart; she had never felt so tall.

"If not for her, could I do this?" Anuradha gestured again and a loud crack of thunder rumbled the earth. The hammering on the walls ceased for the barest of moments, then resumed. A low crying carried down from one of the upstairs rooms; Diti startled out of her nap. There was nothing of the doting great-grandmother left in the woman before her. She wasn't feeling much like the loving aunt at the moment herself. Holding the body of her dead son, she doubted she would feel warm and nurturing ever again. But grief was still far from her. It was as if the goddess stood between her and that emotion.

Anuradha folded her arms with a smirk.

Prithvi held her little son tightly. What was the meaning of this feeling of power flowing through her? What good would it do now even if she could do the things her grandmother could do? It wouldn't bring her son back. Why would Sarsuti fill her with power only when it was too late?

She had said to act, and they would act together. But Prithvi didn't know what that meant. She felt like she had the power to destroy all the nomads clamoring around the city walls, if only she knew how.

"You have no answer?" Anuradha said. She flicked a hand skyward again and another crack of thunder shook the earth.

Just act.

"If not for her," Prithvi said, "could I do this?" She did not know the gestures her grandmother used. She simply raised her arm high into the air. The sky instantly darkened and rain began to fall, hissing against the hot pavement stones.

Prithvi shivered in the suddenly cold wind. She feared she had chosen unwisely. She had seen an image in her mind, of rains falling on the mountains for days on end, overflowing the streams, over-flowing the river. How could she have unleashed that in just this instant?

She turned to look at her statue of Sarsuti, but it was still the dark mother gracing the pedestal, sword raised high to cut away what had been outgrown.

"Will you use your power to smite me?" Anuradha taunted over the roar of the rain.

"I won't have to," Prithvi said. The drunken feeling was fading fast. "I think I just smited us all."

"A little rain won't harm us," Anuradha said.

"Not a little, no," Prithvi said. "But I can feel it coming, the water. All we've been missing all these years. It's coming all at once."

"Nonsense," Anuradha said, but the rain pounded down harder than ever.

"They've stopped attacking the walls," Prithvi said.

"How can you tell? It's impossible to hear anything."

"I know they have. We have to get upstairs, all the way to the roof. Now!"

"No," Anuradha said. "I can undo this. The dark mother and I, we act as one." She turned to the statue and began singing and gesturing.

"Look! The water has already filled the courtyard. It will be spilling into this room in a moment. We have to go!"

Anuradha paused only long enough to say, "You go! Take Diti!" Then she resumed her singing, heedless of the water already licking at her heels.

Prithvi tucked her son into the folds of her garment the way the women of the People did when they were nursing then raced up the stairs. The rain fell so hard it hurt. But while the drunken feeling had passed out of her, it had left some of the strength behind. She could do this. She could get Diti up to the roof.

Diti was sobbing and did not sooth when Prithvi picked her up, but the rain was so loud she could scarcely be heard. Prithvi gathered up the blanket from the bed, then went to her own chest, tossing aside clothing and jewelry until she reached the small wooden amulet hidden on the bottom. Clutching it in her hand, she carried her dead son and Diti both up to the roof, covering them all with the blanket as best she could.

The water rose unbelievably fast, too fast to just be from the rain, as torrential as it was. Her sense had been right; this water was flowing down from the mountains, too much all at once. Sarsuti was over-flowing her banks. She was even overflowing the banks she had once reached in her greatest hour; she was filling the city itself. Through the gray sheet of rain Prithvi could see other rooftops rapidly becoming islands all around her. Her house was one of the tallest; perhaps she and Diti would be all right.

She could hear voices around her, sometimes, crying out. Many of the People were not all right.

Prithvi peeled back the edge of the sling and looked again at her son. She could see his father in him, in the curl of his hair and the shape of his face. He was exactly what she had asked for, a gift she had never been allowed to have. She had known when she had called to the goddess that there would be a price, but the price of a thing shouldn't be the thing itself. Not even a dark mother could be so cruel. Prithvi ducked her head, pressing her cheek's to her unnamed son's. The sound of her sobs was lost in the roar of water around her.

The gray dark of day became the absolute dark of night and still the rain continued. Prithvi let Diti nurse, a relief to them both. Then the little girl went to sleep, fussing now and again as the wind changed direction and blew fresh water droplets onto her face. Prithvi was afraid to lay down, afraid to lessen her hold on either of the children, living or dead, for even a moment. The water level was rising more slowly now, but it was still rising.

Had Sarsuti swept the nomads away?

Sometime near dawn the rain finally ended. Prithvi didn't see it; she had already fallen into an exhausted sleep.

She had spent a sleepless night up on the roof once before, with Kochai. It had been their only night, and the gradual lightening of dawn had not been a welcome sight.

"Why did you go to the ocean?" Prithvi, snuggled warm in his arms despite the chill autumn air, had asked.

"My grandfather was a trader from the ocean cities. When he met my grandmother up in the highlands of my home he vowed to be a trader no more, but to stay forever among her people if she would have him. And so he did; he lived out his days never seeing the ocean again."

"So you went to see his ocean?"

"Yes, and it was... indescribable. Water, as far as the eye can see. Flat, blue-gray, going on forever." He had laughed, a rumble in the ear she had kept close to his chest. "I'm afraid I'm a mountain boy at heart. I did not care for it. But the real reason I went was to lay his bones at rest. Among my people when someone dies we bury their bones in their homeland so that they can always look after their tribe, to lend it strength. So I brought grandfather back to his own homeland, to bury his bones there, among his own tribe."

"That's a long journey."

"When I finally reach home again it will be nearly two years since I've last seen my family. But my grandfather was a good man. I could do no less for him."

Prithvi had smiled, and something else, something inside of her or maybe just the hint of something, had smiled as well.

———

Prithvi woke when Diti started to fuss. She wanted at the other breast, the one her son was still tied close to. Prithvi loosened the cloth, moving him gently to her other arm. Diti greedily latched on the moment he was out of the way and Prithvi caught her breath at the fierce tugging. It eased a little when she had the girl in a more comfortable position, but Mara had never mentioned how greedily this girl suckled. But then Mara seldom complained.

Realizing the rain had stopped, Prithvi threw back the blanket. Kochai's words came back: water as far as the eye could see. She didn't like it either. Perhaps that was because her home was now at the bottom of it. It would drain away eventually; once upon a time Sarsuti had overrun her banks often and the streets of the city were built to let the water run through and away, away to the ocean. The buildings would still stand, but the things inside would be ruined or just gone. As would the People.

Prithvi shaded her eyes against the bright sun and looked around. There were other rooftops, but they were all barren. She felt achy and tired. This time when Diti nodded off she made a little nest out of the now sundried blanket and nestled her into it, carefully draping part of it over Diti's face to protect her from the sun. Then she laid down herself, next to her son.

He had never had a name. It would be bad luck to give him one now, at least among the People. His father's tribe might have different traditions. She did know what she had to do now; she had to take him to his father's homeland, to lay his little bones to rest where he could stay forever with his tribe.

She still held the little wooden amulet in her hand, her only remembrance of Kochai. She let it dangle from the long leather cord for a moment, gazing again at the twisting shape carved into it that meant nothing to her. It looked like a sign of protection, or identification with a tribe. She gently wrapped the cord over and over around her son's wrist, then tied it securely.

She remembered Anuradha singing before the dark mother. Had she truly believed that killing every boy child was a good, virtuous thing? She wanted to be scornful, but the feeling wouldn't come. She remembered too well calling upon the rain that quickly became this flood. She had been unsure what to do before, she was unsure now whether it had been the right thing, but she knew that in that moment she had been certain she was doing exactly what Sarsuti wished.

Prithvi must have fallen asleep again because the next thing she knew someone was shaking her awake. The sun was low on the horizon, glinting brightly against the water. Prithvi felt terrible, still achy but now powerfully thirsty as well. Then she looked up and saw her brother, alive and at her side. A rush of happiness ran through her, but quickly turned to sorrow at everything that had happened since last they'd met.

"Oh Daksha," she cried, letting him pull her up into a tight embrace. "My son."

"Yes, I see him," Daksha said. "I'm sorry."

Prithvi wanted to weep, but tears would not come. At last she pulled away and saw Mara sitting on the blanket nest, humming as she nursed Diti. She had no shortage of tears, but they were all happy ones.

"We were on the wall," Daksha said. "The nomads had broken through and were running like madmen through the streets, tearing through houses without even looking for anything, chasing the women. There were only five men of the People left, including me. It seemed all was lost."

"When the rain and the water came we cheered," Mara said softly. "We thought at last Sarsuti was coming to save us from our attackers. And the water raced through the streets, sweeping them all away. But it swept the People away as well. And it moved fast. People would hit walls with such force. No one could..." She broke off, holding Diti tighter.

"Then we could see that the water was going to get higher than the walls and we were truly afraid. I had Mara with me. We tried to get home, running along the wall to the nearest point to your house, but there was no way to cross the streets. They were flooded with angry water."

"Then the water surged and we all were carried away. It was dark then, nighttime I think, but it was raining so hard. But Daksha never let me go."

"I caught hold of a passing building and pulled us both onto the roof. But there was no one else in reach. We thought we two were the only ones left."

"I was afraid it was just me," Prithvi said. "Me and Diti."

"We had to swim to get here. The water looks calm from here, but it pulls. I think by tomorrow someone from one of the fishing villages upriver will come pick us up," Daksha said.

"We saw boats in the distance this morning," Mara added. "Surely by tomorrow they will come to see what remains of our city. Four people and a wasteland of rubble."

"There may be others still," Daksha said, looking about as if hoping to catch sight of one. "We will build again. We are the People, what else can we do?"

Prithvi let the two plan. It kept their minds off their growing hunger, surely. But she said nothing. She knew she would not be staying, not here and not in the fishing village. She had her son's bones to bury, but it was more than that.

She didn't want to share with them the story of what had happened to her, of what Anuradha had done, had been doing for so many years, not even what she had been trying to do at the end. And she didn't want to share what she herself had done.

She wasn't even sure if she had really done those things. Everything from the moment she had started birthing her son until waking up just now was a haze, like a dream. But no, it was too vivid for a dream. It was like remembering something she hadn't actually done, only imagined doing.

But that wasn't it either. She knew she had done those things, she just didn't feel it. For a moment she wished Anuradha were there to talk to, but she quickly dismissed that thought. Whatever power Anuradha had had, it had never come from Sarsuti. But someone, somewhere must know where that power had come from. Where Prithvi's power had come from. In one of the cities that still bustled with life, perhaps she could find a woman with a story like her own.

And maybe, if they talked, Prithvi would know for sure whether she had in a fit of anger destroyed the remains of her People, or if she had merely been a vessel for a greater anger. Until that day, she would hold her tears inside, unshed. And she would never call another place home.

TALE OF A FOX

For the first time in four years of marriage, Asuka did not find her husband's awkward manner and shy smiles endearing. She watched in annoyance as Masuyo got to his feet in a lurch, the movement too hurried to be graceful, and then entangled himself in his long sleeves. The bunkan sokutai she had so carefully fashioned for him was wrinkled, all of her long work wasted by his carelessness.

He would not last a day in Heian-kyo.

Asuka bit the inside of her cheek, willing the tears not to come as Masuyo paid his respects to her father and left. She remained seated where she had so carefully positioned herself earlier, to greet her husband in a rare daytime visit.

She had been glowing with happiness when she had received his message and had extended her invitation to come to call. It had seemed the perfect occasion to show off her new juni-hito, her robes of twelve layers. Each layer was a different color: scarlet, gold, reddish brown, shades of green. They perfectly reflected the colors of the maple leaves that covered the mountains behind her. She had chosen her spot well, the long robes carefully draped until she was like an autumn-colored mountain herself. She had even written a poem for the occasion but had never gotten the chance to recite it.

Masuyo, being Masuyo, had noticed none of her efforts. He had spoken of nothing but his own news. He had been accepted by the Onmyo. Soon he would go to Heian-kyo to join the order and continue his study of yin-yang magic.

And Asuka would be left behind in Nagano.

"And so I lose my son-in-law and heir," her father said as he returned from seeing her husband out. "He will need a new father-in-law in Heian-kyo, one who can help him advance his career."

"Perhaps not," she said. "The Onmyo is different than other branches of Imperial service. Rank does not matter as much as skill, and Masuyo is a very skilled onmyoji. But even if he does marry again, I will always be his first wife. The other will just be a consort."

"What good is that? It's merely a title, *first wife*," her father grumbled. "And you with no child; you are easy to leave behind. Four years of marriage and no child; you must be doing something wrong."

Asuka bowed her head under her fierce gaze. "I'm only sixteen. There is still time for me to have a child."

"Not if you're in Nagano and your husband is in Heian-kyo." He turned to leave but paused in the doorway, not quite looking back at her as he said, "You had best make good use of the time you have left before he leaves. I expect a grandchild."

"Yes, father." But he had already gone.

Asuka rose in one smooth motion, the many layers of her robes falling into perfect arrangement with no visible effort on her part, and walked along the garden to her room, the end of her long, black hair whispering along the floorboards behind her.

She went to a lacquered box in the corner and took out the first poem Masuyo had written for her, before they were married. Being a scholar he had written it in Chinese characters, which she could not read, but she knew the words by heart. She had cherished it for years. She had always imagined she could see his love glowing from the calligraphy. Now she wondered, was it a man's love for a woman she saw, or a poet's love for his own words?

Asuka put the poem away with a sigh then took out another. This one was written in a scrawl on rough brown paper. No perfume had adorned it, no sprig from a cherry tree. She had never answered it, for what lady would reply to such a coarse overture? But she had never thrown it away either. And if the stories about Nakamura Katashi were true, he might be her only hope now.

Asuka rubbed ink on her inkstone and began composing a reply four years in the waiting.

Nakamura Katashi came to call the very next day. Asuka arranged herself as carefully as she had the day before even though, not being her husband, all Katashi would see of her would be an outline on a screen. She did not mind being hidden, it was only proper, but she did wish that she could see him. She wanted to see his face, to examine his features. Even though he had pursued her as a marriage prospect she had never seen him. Would there be something vulpine in his eyes or in the shape of his nose or mouth? It was said he disdained make-up; through the screen all she could tell was that he had no hat. Such an odd man; surely the stories were true.

"Good morning, Lady Asuka," he said as he settled himself before her screen.

"Good morning, Nakamura Katashi. Thank you for seeing me so quickly."

"Punctuality is a virtue, one I'm sure you prize, my lady," he said. She couldn't tell if he was mocking her or not.

"My husband," she said, "has received an appointment to the Onmyo."

"So I've heard. He is well suited for such a career." This time she was certain he was mocking her.

'You do not think much of the Onmyo, do you, Nakamura Katashi?"

"Or your husband," he added.

Asuka blinked at that blatant insult. This conversation was not going as planned. "They say the famous onmyoji Abe no Seimei had incredible powers."

"So they say."

"They say it is because his mother was a kitsune, a fox spirit," Asuka went on. Hidden in the large sleeves of her juni-hito her hands clenched tight.

"I have heard that as well," Katashi said. Asuka studied his shadow on her screen, the tone of his voice. Was he challenging her?

"I have heard the same about you, Nakamura Katashi," she said, hands clenching tighter. If he took offense and left, there was nothing she could do to bring him back.

"Yes, I assumed you knew that. Who else would you wait four years to answer my letter?" Asuka almost chided him for the disgraceful state of his letter, the bad poetry and childish calligraphy, the poor attention to details like the quality of paper and ink. But she needed his help, so she held her tongue.

"Are the stories true? Was your mother a kitsune?" she asked instead.

"It's a convenient story to attach to a motherless child, isn't it? For something as unnatural as a mother leaving her husband and infant son, an unnatural explanation is best, it seems. But why don't you ask me what you summoned me here to ask me?"

That answer did not satisfy her at all. It almost sounded as if he were saying he wasn't a kitsune. "What I ask for can only be done by someone of great magic," she said.

"So ask." He was beginning to sound impatient, and Asuka accepted that this was as much of an answer as she was likely to get.

"My husband is to leave for Heian-kyo soon, but I do not wish him to go. I wish him to stay were with me in Nagano."

"As a good Buddhist, shouldn't you just let him go? Accept it as the transitory nature of life, like cherry blossoms. Beautiful while they last, which is measured in days. You were married in cherry blossom season. I know, I remember. You were quite lovely."

That was impertinent, to imply he had actually seen her. "The one has nothing to do with the other," Asuka said. "All I need to know is, can you make this happen?"

"It's no small thing you ask," he said.

"Yes, but can you do it? I don't care how, as long as he stays with me."

"It can be done," he said. "But what would you give me in return?"

"Anything," she said without hesitation. Despite her hopes, she had been afraid that he would deny being a kitsune or would refuse her request. She had not spared a thought about what she would do if he said yes.

To her great surprise he lifted her screen and passed under it. Asuka jumped and scrambled back across the floor, tangling herself in the layers of her juni-hito. She went sprawling with a most undignified thump. Katashi leaned over her, his eyes gleaming with impish delight. Now that she had seen him, she could never doubt the stories. He was all fox.

Katashi reached out and drew one finger down the side of her face then lifted it before his eyes and rubbed it against his thumb.

"I wonder, what do you really look like, under all this?" he said as white powder fell from his fingertips, dusting the silk of her robes.

"How can you ask such a thing?" she gasped, managing to untangle herself enough to sit up. "Unless that's your payment? To see me without make-up?"

"Hardly," he said, amusement dancing in his eyes. "But partly."

"Will you do what I ask?"

"I will think on it," he said, getting to his feet.

"When can I expect your answer?"

"Soon."

On the whole, a most unsatisfactory interview.

Masuyo came to her room that night, and she did her best to follow her father's advice. She had no other sisters; if her husband left her without children, her father would have no heirs.

"I checked the auguries for the most auspicious time for my departure," Masuyo told her as he stumbled about her room collecting his things by the gray light of dawn. "I will be leaving at sunset by the south pass."

Asuka bit her lip. She had not yet heard from Katashi, and now time was shorter than she had thought. Nothing she could say would make Masuyo delay an action that the auguries had already indicated, so she did not answer, merely shivered and burrowed deeper under her covers. It was cold, much colder than usual for so early in the autumn.

Fully dressed at last, Masuyo slid open the door between her room and the garden, but he did not step outside. Asuka turned and sat up. He was standing motionless with one hand on the doorframe.

"Were the auguries wrong?" she asked mischievously.

"I… don't know. How can this be?"

Since he didn't seem likely to explain anything, Asuka climbed out of her warm bed and crossed the room to stand behind him.

Her garden was buried in snow and more was falling, great thick flakes spiraling down from the star-filled sky in eerie silence.

Katashi had sent his answer.

———

Masuyo had been certain that such an early snow would quickly melt, but he was wrong. Each night brought a fresh layer of snow until soon the people of Nagano had to dig tunnels to get out of their homes.

Masuyo spent more time with Asuka than he had since the first few months of their marriage, but she soon grew tired of his visits. If he wasn't complaining of how incompetent the few onmyoji in Nagano were – both in ridding the city of the clearly unnatural weather and in mentoring his further studies – he was composing poems about butterflies unable to escape their cocoons.

Asuka had not heard from Katashi since the snow had begun to fall, but every night when Masuyo wasn't there she dreamed of him. The dreams were so vivid she woke expecting to find his warm body next to hers, or marks on her body, or at least her nightclothes to be in disarray. But there were no signs, so they must be dreams. And yet why didn't the dreams come when Masuyo was there?

One evening Asuka offered to play the flute for Masuyo just to stop his endless complaining. He reclined, sipping warm sake to fight the chill, but she hardly noticed him, lost as she was in her own music.

"What song was that?" Masuyo asked when she had finished.

"It's called the song of seasons," she said.

"The song of the seasons? Why do you play it so slow? It sounds like a dirge. That will never bring on spring."

"Who cares about spring?" Asuka asked, feeling petulant after his criticisms of her flute playing. "Don't you think the snow is lovely when it falls from a clear sky?"

"That lovely snow is blocking all of the passes out of Nagano," he said.

"And trapping you here with me," she finished for him. He gaped at her in what she slowly realized was genuine shock.

"Asuka, my being stuck here is only the smallest part of it. No one can get out, but no one can get in either. That includes supply wagons. The snow fell before the harvest was brought in. Nagano is starving. You don't see it spending every day within the confines of your mansion, but I do. And if we don't get an early spring, many people will die."

Asuka had never before felt trapped in her life, perhaps because she had never before had reason to want to leave the walls of her home aside from short trips in a carriage to the shrine on the mountaintop. Although she still dreamed of Katashi, he did not answer any of the letters she sent him. She tried staying awake all night in case they weren't truly dreams but dozed off shortly before dawn, then dreamed. And in her dreams, she could never speak.

But she knew where Katashi lived. She passed his house in her carriage every time she visited the shrine. It was beyond the outskirts of the city at the edge of the forest, just off the road that went up the mountain to the shrine.

So on a night when Masuyo did not come, she dressed in her warmest juni-hito, slipped out of the house while her father and servants were sleeping, and started walking along the road that would eventually take her to Katashi.

Asuka had taken a pair of wooden sandals that belonged to one of the servants, the tallest pair she could find. But they were designed for rain and mud, not snow so deep it was past her hips in some places.

"Oni soto, fuku wa uchi. Oni soto, fuku wa uchi," she chanted under her breath as she trudged. Her father had said those words just that morning as he threw roasted soybeans out the door. "Demons out, luck in." Had she imagined it, or had he shot her an accusing look as he had stepped back inside the house? No one in Nagano felt like celebrating Setsubun but like her father they were going through the motions. Whether she had imagined that look or not, Asuka was certain only she could get the demons out.

She had never been so cold. She could not feel her hands or feet or, more distressingly, her face. The wind kept changing directions, keeping her hair and clothes constantly twisting around her. At least the snow was not so deep outside of the city. She kept her head down – easier than trying to keep her hair out of her eyes – and kept putting one foot in front of the other. She continued chanting until the words were no more than meaningless syllables.

She was beginning to feel warm again, warm and sleepy, when the strap on one of her sandals broke and she went sprawling into the snow. When she finally managed to sit up and look around she was surprised by two things. First, she must have overshot Katashi's house because she was deep in the woods now; second, she had fallen into the midst of the biggest skulk of foxes she had ever seen. There had to be nearly fifty of them; some white, some red, all gazing at her in complete unconcern.

"Kitsune?" she said, straightening her sodden robes and hair into some semblance of order. "Are you kitsune? Please, I need help. I'm lost."

The foxes did not move. With a sigh, Asuka got back to her feet and turned to retrace her steps. Standing behind her was a statuesque woman with a face as pale and cold as the moon.

"You wish to find Katashi?" the woman asked. Her lips barely seemed to move when she spoke, but her voice was clear.

"Yes!" Asuka said.

"I can take you to him, but what will you do for me in return?"

"Anything!"

The woman laughed. "I see you've learned nothing about dealing with kitsune," she said. Asuka's cheeks burned.

"Pardon me for asking, but are you Katashi's mother?" she asked.

"No. That one would not help you."

"But you do know Katashi?"

The woman did not answer, but the barest hint of a smile touched her lips. "Come," she said at last. "I will take you to Katashi."

"And in return?" Asuka asked, hoping it wasn't too late to be sensible.

"Don't worry. What I have in mind will serve both our interests."

Asuka was expecting more of an explanation, but she wasn't going to get it. She took a step and nearly fell again before she remembered her broken sandal. She slipped her feet out of both of them, but when she looked up again the lady was once more a fox.

The fox jogged soundlessly over the snow and Asuka stumbled and ran and stumbled again trying to keep up. It seemed like they ran further than she had walked before. Then she tripped over a tree root and fell face-first into a snow drift. By the time she had struggled free of the soft snow the fox was nowhere to be seen.

Asuka flopped back into the snow, too exhausted to go on. Surely the kitsune would come back for her. She looked up at the tree towering over her, a plum tree. Was that snow on the ends of its branches, or was it already covered in white blossoms?

What happened next made so little sense that Asuka was sure she must be dreaming. How else could she explain a plum tree picking her up out of the snow and carrying her into Katashi's house? The tree plunged her into a tub of steaming water. She had never been immersed in water before and she panicked, but she didn't have the strength left to translate that panic into more than the weakest of motion in her limbs. The warmth of the water made her aware once more of how cold she was, down in her bones. She couldn't stop shaking.

But slowly the bath warmed her all the way down and her shivers slowed then stopped. She was just beginning to enjoy soaking in the water when the plum tree plunged her head under the surface. She flailed and fought until the touch of cloth on her face startled her. He was just washing away her make-up.

He, for now the tree had become Katashi. And somewhere in the dream time she had lost her clothes. All twelve layers of them.

"What are you doing?" she asked.

"Warming you up. I know how you aristocrats feel about bathing, but it really is necessary. I suppose your husband told you it was an inauspicious day for getting wet?"

"No," Asuka said. Her mind felt like it was still frozen, her thoughts came so slowly.

"It's a shame there is nothing we can do about your teeth but wait for the stain to fade," Katashi grumbled.

"You're an aristocrat too," Asuka said. "You may be of the lowest rank, but you're still an aristocrat. You should have some standards."

"Standards of beauty you mean?" he said. "Trying to take one moment in time and make it last forever? And that one moment is an illusion anyway? No, thank you. I can see an old woman making herself look young again, but why a young woman wishes to look like she's already lost all her teeth is beyond me. But then, I have no desire to live in Heian-kyo."

"Nor do I," Asuka admitted, twisting the washcloth in her hands. "Not that I have a choice. But even if I did, I wouldn't want to go. I'm too provincial; the city women would not accept me."

"Would you mind telling me what you were doing freezing to death in my garden?"

"A kitsune in the woods led me here. A woman, not your mother."

"Ah. And you were in the woods because…"

"Because you wouldn't answer my letters. This unnatural winter needs to end. I'm sorry I ever entered into an agreement with you. There must be some way to negate it."

"I like the winter," Katashi said.

"The people are starving."

"I find that amusing, actually. They live in a valley teeming with game and yet they are starving."

"We're Buddhists! We can't hunt!" Asuka said.

"That's not my problem," he said. "You wanted your husband to remain in Nagano, and he remains in Nagano. You said you didn't care how I did it."

"I regret it. Didn't I say I regret it? What will it take to make it end?" Asuka was shivering again. The water was growing cold.

"That would be up to me, wouldn't it? And I choose not to end it. In future, be more careful in what you say when making bargains."

"Never trust a fox," Asuka mumbled under her breath. "Where are my clothes? I need to be home before anyone notices I'm gone. My reputation would not survive being found at your house."

"Indeed," he agreed. "But there is the little matter of your end of the bargain."

"Haven't I repaid you?" Asuka asked, still unsure whether she had dreamed his nightly visits.

"Do you think you have?"

"I don't know," she admitted.

Katashi flashed that smile once more. "Time to get out of the tub."

"My clothes?"

"You aristocrats with your aversion to nudity. If you weren't all so fat, it wouldn't bother you so much," Katashi grumbled. "I'll make one last bargain with you. For the sake of your sensibilities, I'll leave my clothes on."

He reached out a hand to help her from the tub. Asuka took it. She had long practice in letting her mind run while her body went through all the elegant motions of ritual, and what was this but another ritual? And her mind *was* running, for Katashi had just given up his secret. And she understood what the kitsune in the forest had meant, and how she could serve both their interests.

———

She made quite a sight wandering down the road from the shrine, bare feet caked in mud from puddles of melting snow, her knotted and snarled hair dragging over the ground behind her, her silk robes dirty and torn. But Asuka knew more than most about the power of presentation; her appearance was as carefully planned as it had been on her wedding day.

The first people to see her spread the word and by the time she reached her father's house there was a crowd following with her. They asked frantic questions, but she ignored them all, walking with the practiced grace of a lifelong aristocrat. When her father and Masuyo came racing down the street to meet her she swooned. And for once her husband didn't disappoint her but caught her and swooped her up into his arms, an image the crowd would remember when they later heard her tale.

Asuka laid abed for three days listening to the sound of the water drip, drip, dripping in her garden and not speaking to anyone. On the fourth day Masuyo came to call, bringing the other Nagano onmyoji with him, and Asuka knew it was time to talk.

"I was possessed," she said, "by a fox spirit."

The three onmyoji gasped. One produced a fresh scroll from the sleeve of his bunkan sokutai and sat down at her writing table to take notes.

"How did this happen?" Masuyo asked.

"It was because of Nakamura Katashi."

"Ah!" the oldest onmyoji cried. "So he is a kitsune!"

"Yes, but he was not the kitsune who possessed me," Asuka said. "It was the others."

"The others?"

"There are many kitsune in the forest around Nagano," Asuka said, remembering the skulk of foxes she had come upon. She didn't really know if they had been kitsune or just ordinary foxes, but her tale was taking on a life of is own. "But you shouldn't be alarmed; they are there to help us."

"But the snow…"

"Was the work of Nakamura Katashi," Asuka said, truthfully enough. "The others were angry with him for that. That is why they possessed me. They sent me to his house to stop him."

"Stop him? How?" Masuyo asked. He looked more concerned than suspicious. She had spent the night at another man's house, but even her husband believed she had been possessed.

"I…" Asuka paused, overcome. She dropped her head, letting her hair slide over her face.

"You exposed him," the oldest onmyoji said matter-of-factly. "You found his tail and exposed him for the fox he was."

Asuka nodded glumly. "I believe that is what happened. My memories are muddled."

"That is to be expected," the onmyoji said, "When one is possessed by a fox."

"Will she be all right?" Masuyo asked.

"She seems fine now."

"You have broken the spell that held Nagano," the note-taking onmyoji declared. "My lady, we are grateful."

Asuka managed the correct, polite smile. Soon her husband would leave her, but the thought no longer troubled her. For although it was perhaps too soon for most women to tell, Asuka was sure she could already sense the little one growing within her.

And if in nine months she bore a child that had something distinctly vulpine in its features, who was to criticize her? She was the heroine of Nagano. And she had, after all, been possessed by a fox.

FULL CIRCLE

April wondered if the puppy wasn't more trouble than he was worth. It was a typical Mom gift, unasked for and exceedingly high maintenance. She could have at least found one that was already housebroken. This one had clearly been born somewhere with gravity. He kept trying to squat in the corner, which only sent him flying across the cockpit, little golden globules streaming behind him. Or worse.

"Come on, Boo. I don't want to stand here all day," she grumbled. At last the puppy's wigglings quieted momentarily. She could feel the muscles of his abdomen working under her hands. Then the wiggling resumed and she switched off the suction and lifted him away from the vacuum hatch that served as his toilet. High maintenance. But if she didn't help him go now, he was sure to go on Tony and Rosa's shuttle. And Rosa was just as sure to have a fit.

She was nervous enough about the trip. Tony had asked her to stop by just to say hello, but she wasn't fooled. She knew he was going to ask her yet again to do a job for him. She had done so many jobs for him while still living with her mother she couldn't seem to make him see she wasn't interested in that line of work anymore.

It had always been a sham. How could he have such confidence in her abilities as an exorcist? She had told him flat out she didn't believe in ghosts. Yet he kept calling. And she owed him so much, she kept answering his calls.

Tony's home was an ever-changing amalgam of borderline space-worthy vessels. As members of his extended family came and went so did some of the ships, but there were never less than ten tethered together. April saw a new acquisition, a Class III shuttle, the kind with the very latest in radiation shielding. Very nice. There didn't seem to be any sign of damage, none of the hasty patches that the other ships had. She wondered how it had come to be abandoned.

After donning her spacesuit and stuffing Boo into his pressurized carrier, she hooked her ship's tether to her belt and jumped over to Tony's ship. Once, when she was a very young girl, before her mother's life had fallen apart, she had been on a ship that had docked with another ship, and she had crossed from one to the other through the airlocks, just like floating down a hallway. But that was for rich folks. Poor folks just hopped through the blackness of space.

She landed with practiced ease on the hull of the largest ship, locking the end of her tether onto one of countless rungs. She made her way to the cargo bay, towing Boo's carrier behind her. Someone must have been watching her approach, because as soon as she was inside the cargo bay the doors closed. Through her helmet she could faintly hear the hiss of air filling the space. She was just pulling off her helmet when Rosa sailed in to greet her.

"April! It's so good to see you!"

"Likewise."

"Are you hungry?" Always the first words out of Rosa's mouth.

"I could eat."

"You could eat! Girl, you're barely more than skin and bone. When was the last time you had something to eat that wasn't synthetic protein?"

"That would be the last time I was here," April admitted. She couldn't help grinning. Tony and Rosa's shuttle was nicer than most - the original hull to slapdash patch-job ratio was very high – but putting a proper kitchen inside of a shuttle was generally regarded as insanity. Living in space, one was always aware of the few inches of alloyed metal that held death at bay. The damage a sudden explosion could do was never far from mind either. But Rosa said a home wasn't a home if there wasn't a kitchen. One did not use the word "microwave" in her hearing. There was a difference between heating up food and cooking it, she said. April agreed with her.

"You let that puppy out to gambol and come inside. Tony is waiting to see you."

"Yes, ma'am." April lifted the latch on the carrier and Boo bounded out, propelling across the cargo bay. April caught him, his little legs doggy-paddling madly, and redirected him towards the door.

When they reached the dining area, Tony and another man were already eating. Rosa put a "plate" together for her as Tony tried to squeeze the life out of her in a bear hug. Then April buckled into a chair and Rosa passed her an enclosed tray of food. Rosa had a dim view of people pecking food out of the air, eating like fish. April tucked into her food with a gusto that bordered on the impolite. Rosa's words to the contrary it was still mostly synthetic protein, but it was hot and spicy synthetic protein with a generous helping of Rosa's famous kimchee. To April, it was ambrosia.

"April, do you know Lee?" Tony asked. "He's married to my sister Yolanda."

"We've never met," Lee answered for her, as her mouth was full of food. She swallowed, smiled, and reached across the table to shake the hand he was offering her.

"Lee just got back from a salvage mission out near the Belt," Tony said. "He picked up some corporate broadcasts on his way back to us."

"The rumors are true," Lee said, picking up the story. "They've found an Earth-like planet."

"Who found?" April asked.

"Some consortium of corporations," Lee said, waving his hands in a vague gesture. "All those acronyms blend for me."

"They've already staked their corporate flags," Tony said as Rosa gathered up the trays before disappearing into the kitchen. "They won't let us into their orbiting space stations. What makes you think they'll share a planet with us?"

"It's good news for mankind," Lee said. April, sensing some father-in-law/son-in-law tension about to spill over, scrambled for some way to change the subject.

"I saw a new shuttle as I was coming in," she said. "Any idea how it came to be abandoned?"

"That's my salvage," Lee said. "The previous owners froze to death when their heaters failed."

"The timing of your visit couldn't be better. Lee needs your help," Tony said.

"Tony, I don't do that anymore," April said.

"Oh, I know you stopped for awhile, sure, but you've got that dog now," Tony said.

"My dog?" April repeated, simultaneously wondering what he was talking about and where the dog in question had gone.

"Your mother told us she sent you that dog to help you with your work," Tony said. "He's sensitive to… what did she call it?"

"Psychic vibrations," Rosa answered.

April sighed and scrubbed at her temples. Of course that was why her mother had sent the dog. She should have known there was a reason.

"If you just go over there and do that thing you do, it will make Yolanda feel so much better," Rosa said.

"I can't," April said. "You know I love you guys. I owe both of you more than I could ever repay. But I just can't do that anymore. It makes me feel so…" she lifted her hands helplessly. She couldn't explain it, and it was plain from the way they were looking at her that they wouldn't understand it even if she could.

"Is this why things didn't work out for you on that derelict station? All that work your mother did to get you a spot on it, and you blew it in only a month," Tony said.

"You know about that?" April had spent one blissful month on that station, a rather large piece of corporate trash that a crew of spacers had pounced on. They had made all sorts of slapdash repairs, making do with what they could find. It had only had half gravity, but it had been heaven. Then one of the two air processors had had a critical failure and the spacers in charge had evicted half of the population without notice, including April.

"They would have kept you if they'd known your skills," Tony said.

"I was a welder. They had lots of welders," April said.

"Did they have lots of exorcists as well?" he asked.

"That station was abandoned after a catastrophic hull breach. Many corporate workers died," Rosa said. "Many ghosts remain."

"I never saw any."

"You never do, dear. But others did, didn't they?" Rosa persisted. "And you turned away."

"But I can't actually *do* anything. It's just a story. A scam, really."

"I know a great many people who would disagree with you there," Tony said. "You don't feel like you're really doing anything. Fine. If it helps, think of it as giving Yolanda peace of mind. That's what we're paying you for."

"All right," April said. "I'll do it." She started to unbuckle from her chair but Rosa stopped her.

"After coffee and dessert, dear," she said. "I'll be back in a jiff."

"I'll find your dog while you eat," Tony offered, drifting out of the room.

"So how'd you come to be an exorcist if you don't believe in ghosts?" Lee asked.

"My mother," April said, "was a huge believer in ghosts. She saw them everywhere. Then one day she got it into her head that I could do something that made them go away. And so a career was born." She didn't add, *when I was seven.*

She couldn't remember now how she had put it all together, what it was that had her mother sobbing in the middle of the night, sometimes even screaming. Certainly the word "ghost" had never come up. But one night it had all been just too much for April.

"Someone make it go away, someone make it go away!" her mother had been sobbing over and over, clutching that battered doll of hers, the one with the purple hood and cape. Only there had been no one else in their little derelict, just the two of them. Her mother's eyes had been bulging, her hands up to ward off blows April couldn't see.

And something in April's head had just snapped.

"Go away!" she had shouted. And apparently it had. Or her mother believed it had, which to April amounted to the same thing.

The image of the doll suddenly held April's attention. She had forgotten that doll. What had her mother called it? She couldn't recall. Some sort of superhero; it had been a toy she had brought with her when she and her own parents had left Earth. It had been a talisman for her mother. It had kept the madness at bay. April had never even been allowed to touch it.

She slowly realized Lee was still talking to her. "It must be quite lucrative in space for someone in your line of work," he was saying. "Everyone living in salvaged ships. Junkers. You know at least one person died in any ship you find."

"Sometimes generations," April said. She resisted the urge to point out that the people taking ships where the prior occupants had all met nasty deaths weren't exactly rich. The rich lived in the big revolving space stations, the ones with artificial gravity, green plants, and real food.

When April finally stepped inside the Class III shuttle, she was pleased to find that Lee had already gotten the basic life support systems up and running. She wasn't sure if Boo could do his job while confined to the carrier, and she particularly didn't want to test it on his first mission solo. If she had to do an exorcist job, she preferred to do it for a friend of Tony's. He always did an excellent job of convincing her clients that she worked better alone. When she had done jobs for her mother she had often had to put on quite the show with various holy relics before the client would believe she had dispelled the spirit. When she was alone, she could fall back on her original method of just shouting "Go away!"

"Well, go to it. Show me the ghosty." She looked at the dog, and the dog looked back at her. Then he pushed off the floor to sail up into her head, a mass of hair and slobber.

"Come on!" she protested, putting a hand between his mouth and her face. "We're on a job here. Show me the ghosty!" She pushed the dog away from her, towards the rest of the ship. His paws caught on the doorframe and he gave himself another push, finally interested in exploring the ship.

April poked around the ship herself, not really expecting to find much. She had been in so many supposedly haunted ships before and never seen anything. She never heard funny noises or felt cold spots. But her mother wasn't the only to act like she saw something that April didn't.

Boo suddenly started howling, insanely loud in the contained space. April followed the sound to the back of the ship. She could see fear and duty wrestling for control of the little dog's mind as he barked then cowered then barked again. The cowering was particularly ineffective in zero G; it was more of a full-body flinch.

April faced the direction that seemed to be bothering Boo the most and raised her hand.

"Go away!" she commanded. As always she felt herself stretching out with her senses, trying to feel something but coming up dry. Boo quieted and April held him close until the last little woofing noises stopped and his shaking limbs relaxed.

"Good work," she murmured to him as she carried him back to the airlock. "Good job, boy."

She was about to seal her helmet when a flash of purple caught the corner of her eye. Something in a crate tucked under a bench. Curious, she reached in and pulled it out.

April felt her own limbs shaking as she saw what it was. It was a doll, a doll she knew very well. Her mother's doll.

"Mom?" She glanced back but of course saw nothing. Even if there had been a ghost, it was gone now. She looked at the doll in her hands. Her mother would have put it in a place of honor, not left it in a crate in what appeared to be a storeroom.

Could there be two such dolls? Or had her mother won the fight against her own madness and no longer needed her talisman?

April zipped the doll into a pocket on her suit and wiped her eyes before sealing her helmet. She might never know for sure; her mother was constantly on the move, and what communications she sent were sporadic and seldom to the point. Like gifts of ghost-hunting dogs.

Or jobs on space stations.

In the meantime, there was still the question of how she was going to get paid for this job. She knew without asking that Lee didn't have any money. What would he offer in trade? He seemed handy; maybe he could upgrade the air cleaners on her own nearly derelict shuttle. With a puppy living with her now she was going to need it.

ON DESPERATE SEAS

t all started with Penelope. Or perhaps really it was Jane, for it was Jane's letter that sent me on the first leg of my improbable journey:

"Dearest Edgar,

Please come at once. Our beloved Penelope has fallen deathly ill."

The letter went on, of course. In typical Jane fashion, she filled a page and a half with the various inadequacies of Dr. Mansley. Only Jane would argue the science at length without ever once considering I might not wish to abandon my own medical practice to return to Newfoundland for the sake of the woman who had broken our betrothal without warning to marry another.

And yet here I was, at their very door.

Jacob answered my knock. His look of shocked surprise told me that Jane had written to me without his knowledge. But the shock quickly melted into a teary gratitude. My extended hand was taken with gusto, and I was quickly led to a place by the fire, a glass of brandy pressed into my hands to warm me after my long walk from town in the cold night.

"Thank God you've come. What did Jane tell you?" he asked as he sank into the chair opposite mine. He was much aged since I had seen him last; too much aged, with deep furrows of grief and worry marring a face I had always thought a jovial one.

"Very little," I allowed. "Only that I am needed."

"More can wait until he has seen her," Jane said from the doorway. With no more greeting than that she took the brandy from me and led me up the stairs to where Penelope lay.

I've been in many sick rooms, and there is a sameness to the smell: a closed-in, concentrated collection of odors, of bile and blood and other less pleasant things. Yet when Jane opened the door to Penelope's room, it was the smell of the sea which assailed me.

"You've left her to sleep with the windows open?" I demanded as I rushed inside.

"Come, Edgar," Jane said. "Even if I had, we are not close enough to the sea to fill the room with the smells of high tide."

I was still puzzling over this when the figure on the bed stirred. "Edgar?" Her voice, her sweet voice. A memory tried to wash over me: our last day together down on the beach between the rocks. The day... the day we...

But I kept my head above water, so to speak. Jane showed me to the chair placed by the bedside then moved about the room lighting lamps until at last I could see her huddled there under the blankets, my one-time fiancée.

It was clear to me at once that she had been ill for quite some time. She was thin and a grayish sort of pale, and all of her golden tresses had been cut away, leaving her with the barest cap of blonde curls. She smiled at me and reached out so I could take her hand, but she was too weak to lift her head, and the hand I clasped in my own was like ice.

"Penelope," I began but realized at once my voice was betraying me. I could not speak to her as a lover, not now that she was another man's wife.

That memory tried to take me again: the sun and wind in her hair, the warmth of her skin, of her lips...

The sea smell was so strong in the room, it was perhaps no wonder it called to mind the beach. It was with some effort I reminded myself of my duties as a doctor. I changed my grip on her hand, pressing my fingers to her wrist to feel her pulse. It was slow but steady.

"What's the matter, specifically?" I asked. "What has Dr. Mansley surmised?"

"He's been quite useless," Jane said, not bothering to hide her scorn. "First he thought pneumonia, then consumption, then some defect in her blood."

"He bled her?" I pulled back the sleeve of Penelope's nightgown. There was indeed a row of healing cuts in her arm.

"He weakened her horribly, very nearly killed her, I think, before Father took my advice and put a stop to it." Penelope seemed to be drifting in and out of sleep, not even bothering to listen to this conversation about her near-death. She was indeed very weak. "Barbaric practice," Jane grumbled.

"Out-dated science," I amended. "Have you tried your own skills on her?"

"Of course," Jane said, almost a rebuke. "No herbal remedy I know has done more than give her a few hours' peace." She moved to the other side of the bed and sat next to her half-sister, winding her fingers through the uneven curls. "I even went myself to Boston to speak with a Chinese herbalist there, but the tincture he gave me has not helped, and no amount of money would bring him to Newfoundland so he could see her himself."

This was startling news. "You went to Boston and back? How long has she been ill?"

"Months. Almost since her husband left. He…"

But Penelope's eyes flew open at the word "husband". The sleepy smiles were gone; now she was wild and terrified.

"Edgar!" she cried, seizing my hand. "He has my heart!"

"What?"

She fought her way up onto one elbow, her sister simultaneously supporting her and trying to quiet her and get her to lie back down. But Penelope would not be quieted.

"He has my heart, Edgar, and he took it with him to the bottom of the sea!" She tore at the neckline of her nightgown, pulling it askew until she could press my captive hand to her breast.

So cold. How could a person yet live with flesh so cold?

Then the chest beneath my palm began to heave.

"Quickly! The basin!" Jane cried, helping her wheezing sister to sit up. I seized the porcelain basin from the nightstand, getting it to Penelope's lap just in time. She heaved again and again, and the smell of the sea became so strong as she vomited I felt I must be drowning.

At last she quieted, slumping against her sister, who stroked her curls and murmured soft nonsense into her ear as I took away the basin.

It was filled with water, green-tinged water. It was surely more than one stomach could contain. I dipped a finger in and licked it: salt water.

Jane was laying the now-quiet Penelope back against the pillows. The nightgown was still askew, the inner curve of her left breast exposed to the lamplight. I saw what my hand had failed to feel: a long silvery scar over her heart. Jane covered her sister up, but not before she knew I had seen.

Penelope roused once more, this time neither sweet nor crazed but melancholy.

"Find my heart, Edgar. Will you do that for me? Will you promise?"

"Yes, Penelope," I said. "I promise."

She smiled, but it was a smile with so much sadness in it, it made my heart ache. Then she took my hand and pressed a kiss to it. Her lips were like ice, but the kiss burned like touching metal on a cold, cold day. I pulled my hand back and tilted it toward the lamp, convinced she must have left a mark. Of course there was none. This was always the effect that Penelope had on me; she made me believe the silliest nonsense.

She was already asleep once more. I waited in the corridor as Jane blew out the lamps.

"You did not summon me for my medical opinion."

"No," she admitted then led me back downstairs to where Jacob waited.

"Well?" he asked. If he had a cap in his hands he'd be twisting it.

His struggle between wanting to hope and not wanting to hope was palpable. I looked over at Jane, but she was no help. She did not even look my way, only settled herself in a chair and pulled some bit of needlework onto her lap. What exactly had I just promised Penelope to do?

"I need to find her husband," I said at last. Jacob nodded, apparently not trusting himself to speak. He turned away from me, looking up at the portrait of Penelope's dead mother that had hung over the mantelpiece for as long as I could remember. It could as easily be a portrait of Penelope herself.

"Edgar hopes his presence will rouse Penelope," Jane said without looking up from her work. "It is not for the last farewell."

"Yes," Jacob said. "But he is so far away."

"How far out to sea does his ship take him?" I should perhaps be ashamed to admit how little I know of the life of a sailor, but it was by my mother's design. My father was lost at sea before I was even born, along with all of her brothers in one great storm. She had vowed I would not follow them.

"He's not out hunting whales this time," Jacob said, at last leaving the portrait to pour himself a measure of brandy and bring another for me. "You are familiar, I trust, with the disappearance of the Sir John Franklin expedition to find the Northwest Passage."

"Who isn't? It's been in all the papers." I sipped at my brandy before remembering perhaps the crucial aspect of this case. "There was a reward for rescue or for information leading to recovery."

"Indeed," Jacob said. "The promise of 20,000 pounds, like Helen's face, is enough to launch a thousand ships, even to those treacherous waters. Patrick left in April, shortly after the advert appeared in the *Toronto Globe*."

April. A good time to head north. Now it was late August. But Jane intruded on my thoughts. "Penelope was afraid. She had had a premonition and didn't want him to go."

Her father scoffed. "I'm afraid to say some things haven't changed since you've been away. Indeed, without your calm reason to temper her, Penelope has grown more superstitious than ever. When Patrick chose not to indulge her this once, she became quite unmanageable. I feared she would do herself some injury."

I thought of the scar, the thin line down the inner curve of her breast. It certainly could not be what she claimed it to be. Yes, it was long enough to remove a heart, but that could not be done without cracking open the rib cage. Had she cut herself, caught up in her own imagings? I couldn't quite believe she would do such a thing, and yet the alternative was even more unthinkable.

"I fear she has," I said at last. Jane fixed me with an inscrutable gaze.

"And what of the seawater?" she asked.

"Ah, there must be an explanation for that," Jacob said before I could speak. "She believes that Patrick has been shipwrecked and drowned, and that his body lies at the bottom of the sea. So she acts as if she had drowned herself. Somehow she is getting a hold of seawater and drinking it for the effect. I don't think she remembers doing it, but what other explanation could there be?"

"What indeed?" Jane said evenly.

"It doesn't matter," I said. "I'll bring her husband back to her. Then we shall see."

"It's too much to ask," Jacob said, getting up to pour another brandy with shaking hands. "It's too late in the year for such a journey."

"She will not last till spring," Jane said. His head dropped low and his shoulders shook.

"I already gave my word to Penelope," I said. "I will risk anything for her."

"Oh, son," he said. "No one would hold you to promises made so long ago, to oaths exchanged..." his breath caught with a hitch and it was a moment before he could speak again. "Penelope broke faith with you."

"Indeed," I agreed. "But I renewed my promise this very night. I will find her husband."

"Lord help me, I won't try to talk you out of it," Jacob said. "Jane will prepare a room for you to stay here tonight. I shall go into town and find you a ship."

"Surely that can wait until morning," I said, acutely aware of all the brandy he had consumed, and of all the dangers between his remote home and the town. The road was not a good one.

"It's not even necessary," Jane said. "There is a ship already waiting for him. The *Margaret Mary*."

"You overstep yourself," Jacob said.

"They were going north anyway, in search of the reward. I merely asked them to stay a few extra days to wait for Edgar. They have need of a ship's surgeon, if you are willing."

"It's better than I could hope for, I'm sure," I said. "I shall depart first thing in the morning."

That night I dreamt of Penelope on the beach, the memory I had held at bay all evening finally conquering me in sleep. I had just received Jacob's blessing and we were newly betrothed when Penelope brought me down the narrow path to the beach where she had been born. She told me the story of how her mother on the passage over from Ireland had suffered through days of labor without release. Her mother was convinced that baby Penelope refused to be born at sea. At the first sight of land her husband, Penelope's father, had begged for them to be put ashore. Everyone on the ship had grown weary of the endless crying and screaming; the captain readily consented.

But his crew was not familiar with the treacherous waters around this beach where I stood, listening to Penelope's tale. The rowboat was turned about then dashed against the rocks. The sailor manning the oars and Penelope's father went under at once; their bodies never even washed ashore. But something in the water had taken hold of her mother and carried her to safety. A selkie, Penelope had said. And the minute her mother's feet had touched the sands of Newfoundland, Penelope had been born.

She took me to the very spot where she had been delivered from her widowed mother by a selkie midwife and laid down upon the sand, pulling me down beside her. I would say she allowed me to take liberties, but in fact she did the taking. I only gave, willingly.

It was not a dream I wished to be having, but at least I did not dream of the end of that day, for by sundown she had been another man's wife. Patrick's wife. The wife of a man she had only just met, and a sailor at that. And now I was going to rescue Patrick, if he even still lived.

A thought flitted through my mind. Perhaps it was all true. Perhaps he *had* taken Penelope's heart. Perhaps he had taken it that very day. Was that how he had stolen her from me? With magic? It would explain what had always been unexplainable to me.

But I didn't really believe it, no more than I believed in selkies rescuing women from the sea and helping them deliver their babies.

I awoke the next morning out of sorts. I did not go to see Penelope or bid farewell to Jane or her father. I slipped out of the house shortly after dawn and walked back to town, inquiring until I found which of the many ships docked there was the *Margaret Mary*. The captain was waiting for me with undisguised impatience, and we were well out to sea before I even reached my cabin.

The *Margaret Mary* was a whaler. She did not have steam engines or steel hulls like Sir John Franklin's ships, but she had a crew accustomed to sailing Arctic waters. The captain, a native Newfoundlander like myself, was a gruff fellow, and after giving me a cursory look-over when I first came aboard promptly dismissed me from his mind.

I sensed at once that Jane had not been entirely truthful, and money probably had changed hands to get the captain to wait for me before heading north. I was introduced to others as the ship's surgeon, but quickly realized the ship had no real need for one. There was precious little for me to do other than stay out of the crew's way.

I soon found myself passing the time in the company of the only other non-sailor aboard, the captain's son Tetqataq, or Teddy as he preferred. Teddy had been born in a native village deep in the Arctic, where he had lived with his mother until his father had come to take him away when he was ten. The captain had introduced him to me as his Arctic expert, although from Teddy's cosmopolitan air and almost foppish taste in clothes I had my doubts as to the extent of his expertise. Still, he was a personable companion with a keen and curious mind who soon devoured all the medical texts I had brought with me and constantly asked questions about my work. I didn't mind. There were far worse ways to pass the dreary, endless hours on a ship.

It was not long before the hours became far less dull. Our ship was swept up by an unseasonably early gale. The crew worked without rest as day and night became indistinguishable. As for me, I confess I was violently ill and was soon so miserable I would have welcomed a watery grave just to escape the heaving of the ship and of my stomach.

I was curled up on the floor of my cabin - praying, perhaps even weeping – when Teddy burst in. He was greatly excited, although I was far too insensible to comprehend his words. He pulled me to my feet, helping me walk out of the cabin and up to the deck of the ship.

The rain and spray from the sea stung like ice, and I felt aware for the first time in days, although the sight of the monstrous waves all around us made me wish I were still insensible. Teddy was shouting, but the wind took his voice before it could reach my ears. Then he pointed.

At first I took it for an angel, this white form standing at the prow of the ship. In the wind and rain she almost seemed to shimmer. Then I heard it, faintly at first then stronger and clearer as the storm began to disperse. The words were in no language I had ever heard, but the song seemed so familiar. I couldn't name it, but I knew it well. Perhaps it was a cradle song sung to me when I was just an infant.

The waves shrank from mountains to hills, the rain and clouds disappeared to reveal the star-filled sky, and the gusting winds settled into one strong wind carrying us swiftly to the north.

At last the song died away and the woman at the prow turned, casting back the hood of her white cloak. It was Jane.

She had been hiding in the hold, in a crate she had had secretly brought aboard days before we set sail. It had made a cramped yet comfortable apartment with food and water enough to last her the entire voyage as well as books to pass the time. Yet it was inconceivable to allow her to stay there any longer, so I gave her my own cabin and strung a hammock in Teddy's cabin for my own use.

"Watch her closely," Teddy warned. "The men are superstitious, but they are practical. As long as the wind is favorable they will leave her be, but if another storm should arise, or any other bit of bad luck no matter how mundane it may seem, she will be blamed."

"And you?" I asked. "Are you not superstitious?"

"Superstition is a fear of what seems unnatural to you," he said after a moment's thought. "Singing to the winds is not unnatural to me."

And what of me? Was it unnatural to me? I wasn't sure. I couldn't bring myself to believe her song had calmed the storm, and I couldn't entertain the thought that Jane would believe so either. Penelope, yes, but not sensible Jane.

I did not get the chance to ask her myself. Once she was settled in my cabin she did not come out of it again. If Teddy were right about the crew, this was merely prudence on her part, but I couldn't shake the feeling she was avoiding me, or rather avoiding explaining her actions to me.

That night I had a dream as vivid as when I had dreamt of Penelope on the beach, only if this dream were a memory it was not a memory of mine.

I dreamt I was walking through snow, trudging and stumbling over drifts that occasionally gave way to patches of bare ice. It wasn't land beneath me; it was sea. I looked around but all I could see were snow and ice glowing softly in the rising sun. Where was land? *Was* there land?

Men walked all around me, heads bent into the wind. I knew them and yet I didn't, like with Jane's song. My heart was heavy in my chest, beating slowly and painfully. I knew this feeling. I had felt it when I had left Newfoundland so many years before. My heart was breaking. I turned to look back, to catch one last glimpse of that which I loved most.

Behind me was a ship caught in the ice. There was another behind her, also trapped. The ice had pushed them up and over so that they listed dreadfully, and despite their steel hulls I doubted they would be seaworthy even if the ice should release them.

I awoke sobbing like a child. Teddy tried to calm me, but I was inconsolable. I didn't know where I was - who I was - I knew only that I had left behind all that I had ever loved, had abandoned her to meet her fate all on her own. Whether this was a ship or a woman I mourned I could not say.

Soft hands brought me out of the dream as merely waking had not.

A mug of tea laced with brandy was pressed into my hands, and as its warmth spread through me I regained my senses.

"Jane," I said, for it was she who had come to my aid, who had answered Teddy's knocking when she had not answered mine.

"Drink it down," she instructed. I took a gulp, swallowed, and began to ask the first of many questions when she interrupted me. "Show me your hand." I did not understand this request, but my hand presented itself of its own accord. Jane took it in hers, turning it this way and that in the lamplight as she examined it closely.

"Here it is," she said, touching the back of my hand, a touch which burned.

"Here what is?" Teddy asked, leaning in closer to see for himself.

"Her mark," Jane said. "Penelope's mark. Her kiss has enspelled you."

"Nonsense," I said, snatching my hand back.

"You don't believe she would?"

"I don't believe she *can*. Spells? Nonsense."

"She's using you to find her husband," she said.

"And why are you here if not to do the same?" I demanded.

"I'm here to keep you safe," Jane said. There was something in her tone of voice, in her eyes as she looked at me... I had seen the change the years had wrought in Jacob and in Penelope, but until that very moment I hadn't realized that Jane was no longer the girl of thirteen she had been the day I had left Newfoundland.

"Tell me what you dreamt. I think it might be significant," she said.

I told it to them in much the same words in which I told it to you. I didn't weep again, but I could still feel the grief as if it were my own.

"Such feelings for a ship," I said. "I don't understand it."

"But then you are not a man of the sea," Teddy said. "That storm we just sailed through was nothing compared to some I've seen. When nothing stands between you and the cold deep but the timbers of your ship... aye, you come to love her. But to sense loss as you describe it, the man must have been her captain."

"Sir John Franklin?" I ventured. I had seen his portrait in the papers, a slightly rotund Englishman, appearing to my eye to be an old gentleman with refined tastes. I doubted very much I had dreamt myself in his place.

"Franklin led the expedition, but the ships had their own captains," Teddy said. "Younger men."

"One was an Irishman," Jane added. Her eyes gazed unseeingly at the ceiling as she searched her memory for the name. "Francis Crozier."

"It sounds familiar," I said. Then gave myself a little shake. "I'm sure I've read it a dozen times in the papers."

"There's something I don't understand," Teddy said. "If Penelope is using you to find her husband, why are you dreaming of the Franklin expedition? Shouldn't you be dreaming of her husband's ship?"

"Patrick's ship was searching for Franklin," Jane said. "The only way to find Patrick is to search for Franklin ourselves."

"I saw nothing that would give us clues in that regard," I said miserably. "Nothing but snow and ice."

"There must have been something else, something you're not noticing," Jane said. "Was there an object that caught your eye? One of the men who seemed more important than the others?"

"No."

"Isn't it possible this was just a dream?" Teddy asked. "Too much worry, things weighing too heavily on your mind."

"You don't believe in magic, Tetqataq?" Jane asked.

"Yes, I do," he admitted. "But it's not my answer to everything." A slow smile spread across Jane's face. Teddy had just risen several levels in her estimation.

Our journey continued on without event. The captain exchanged messages with what ships we passed, but none had heard anything of the fate of the Franklin expedition or of Patrick's ship. Still, we were making excellent time, our wind unfailingly favorable. Jane remained in her cabin, although I would visit her often. We would take meals together, read to each other, or play chess or cards. Sometimes Teddy would join us, but three in a cabin meant for one would quickly grow cramped.

Jane still would not tell me about the song she had been singing in the storm, or why she had sung it, although from time to time we would hear her singing it again, when she was alone in the cabin. She had a lovely voice, but her singing made me uneasy. The crew did not like it either. Teddy had known these men since he was a boy, and they spoke freely with him if not with me. Teddy would tell me the things they whispered to each other, how they thought her singing was responsible for our favorable winds and unseasonably fine weather, but also how her singing was attracting things.

"What sorts of things?" I asked. Teddy shrugged.

"White shapes in the water. Long and immense, but never close enough to the surface to be seen clearly," he replied. "They come up to the ship when she sings, then disappear when she stops."

"Whales?"

"No," he said with a firm shake of his head.

"Have you seen them?" I persisted.

"No, but this crew knows these waters, and they know what is a whale and what is not. If they tell me these things are not whales, then my friend they are not whales."

"I want to see this for myself," I vowed, although my new-found fear of the open water had kept me below decks since the night of the storm. Perhaps it would not be so frightening when the sea was calm, free of waves the size of mountains. I would have to brave it out; secondhand accounts would not satisfy my mind.

It was the middle of the night when she sang again. Teddy and I awoke at the same instant and dashed up to the deck without a word.

"I see nothing," I said after several long minutes of searching. I wondered how anything could be seen in such waters as these; even under the light of a full moon they were black as pitch, so black I expected the waves to leave dark stains as they slapped against the sides of the ship, like a stick dipped in tar.

"Wait," Teddy said, his eyes scanning the waves more calmly than mine. "There," he pointed.

I could see it, although what "it" was I could not say. It was silvery-white like the moon above, but even I knew it was too long and sleek to be a whale.

"Sea serpent?" I pondered, for "serpent" certainly described its shape. "It's longer than our ship."

"Quite a bit longer," Teddy said, as calm as ever. "Depending on how deep it really is."

That thought turned my stomach to rock. Judging from the mumblings of the crew around me, I was not the only one afraid.

The song ended, and the mysterious form dove deeper, fading from view.

"It looked brighter at the front, like its eyes were glowing," I said. Then one of the crew gave a shout I could not quite hear.

"Ice," Teddy said at my look of puzzlement. "Icebergs up ahead. Soon we will be in the Arctic itself."

We went back to our cabin, and I fell back to sleep at once, but it was not a restful sleep. I dreamt I was him again, the Irish captain. I was walking through the snow, pulling a harness like a horse would. My legs below the knees were so numb it was like walking on two peg legs; no feeling of cold, no feeling of the ground beneath me; I was clumsy and slow. The harness around my chest bit deeply; I was pulling something far too heavy for a man to be pulling. It felt like the straps had worn grooves into my flesh; I had been pulling it for a long time.

At first I thought the snow was a bloody pink, as if some massacre had taken place here, but I lifted my gaze and saw *everything* was bloody pink: the snow to the horizon all around, the sky, the other men.

The other men. I wanted to scream at the sight of them but could not make a sound, so I screamed in my own mind, in my own soul. Have you ever screamed such a scream, a scream that does not need to pause for breath?

The men around me were a horror: walking corpses of skin stretched tight over bone; sunken eyes and cheeks making their faces show too much of the skull beneath. The flesh of their cheeks and noses was blackened; some of the men had no noses at all.

It was horrid, but then one spoke to me. I could not hear his voice, but I saw his mouth: a black maw. The teeth were gone and the gums, the tongue, all of it had turned black, blacker even than their faces.

Still they pulled this heavy load, a boat on crude sled runners, over uneven ice and snow. What could be in the boat worth all this?

Nothing. Nothing was worth this. They were in Hell.

I awoke and screamed at last.

Again it was Jane's ministrations that brought me back to sensibility, her gentle yet no-nonsense touch and her tea laced with brandy. I quieted, but my hands still shook as I told them all I had seen.

"Why would Penelope do this to me?" I demanded of Jane. "Why? How can this help?"

"There is something you're meant to see, something small enough where you aren't noticing it," she said.

"Were there any landmarks? Anything that might help us find this place?" Teddy asked.

"No, nothing. Nothing but ice and snow and sky. And men blinded by sun on snow, dying of hunger and scurvy, watching bits of themselves blacken and fall off from frostbite."

"That's horrid," Jane said. She looked repulsed, but I knew my words had not conveyed the true horror of that moment I had lived in that strange man's mind. Those other men, those walking corpses, I had seen madness in their red-rimmed eyes. Their sanity was gone, and I wasn't sure that wasn't a sort of blessing.

The ship's progress was slowed as the icebergs grew larger and more numerous. We met other ships also searching for Franklin near Beechey Island which were preparing to winter over on that desolate shore. There was a cemetery there, just three lone graves, all men from Franklin's expedition, but no clue was found as to the fate of the others. Of Patrick's ship there was still no sign, and the other search ships had seen nothing. They advised waiting for spring but our captain decided to press on.

I was plagued with insomnia. I could not decide whether it would be preferable to dream again of that captain and perhaps finally find the clue Jane thought I should be seeing or to avoid putting myself through another vision of horror. The illusion that I had a choice in the matter kept me awake until the dark hours of early morning, when I would at last fall into a short, dreamless sleep that was far from restful or refreshing. I was beginning to look like a wraith myself.

Then the unthinkable happened. One morning as I slept my fitful sleep, the *Margaret Mary* sailed into Peel Sound. By the time the crew saw the ice, it was too late. I awoke to learn the ship was trapped until such time as the ice chose to release us.

I remembered that first vision I had had of the two ships trapped in the ice. The *Terror* and the *Erebus* had been steam-heated with desalinators for making seawater drinkable and enough canned food to last for years, and still the crew had been forced to walk away and abandon those fine ships. We who had none of those things, when would we be forced to try our chances on foot out on the open Arctic?

It is not surprising the crew turned to Jane when looking for someone to blame. They had left Newfoundland under-equipped and too late in the year and had only made it this far because of the fair weather which they credited her for. They had gambled on their own skill to see them through and had lost. But the option of blaming witchcraft for their fate rather than their own bad planning was too tempting. Nothing could be done about the coming of winter and its weeks of endless night, nothing could be done about the small store of food that was completely inadequate to the task of feeding the crew until spring. But witchcraft? There was always something to be done about that. If you think we are too civilized in 1854 to allow such things to happen, all I can tell you is we were very far from civilization.

Teddy and I were roused from sleep by the sounds of Jane's screams. Before we could even get to our feet our cabin was filled with the grabbing hands of crewmen. Teddy tried to fight but was quickly cuffed on the head, and his hands were tied behind his back before he could recover his senses. I struggled as best I could, but soon I too was bound in chafing rope and hauled up on deck.

The crew had worked fast; they already had made a pyre out on the ice from every scrap of wood they could spare, with one long timber standing at its heart, pointing up to the indifferent sky. The captain was nowhere to be seen, although whether he was turning a blind eye to the proceedings or whether the crew had killed or incapacitated him first I cannot say; even now I do not know.

The crewmen forced me to my knees near the pyre. Teddy was dumped in the snow next to me. He lay motionless, and his face was a wash of blood. I knew well how much even a small cut to the scalp could bleed, but still his lack of movement worried me.

Then Jane was brought out of the ship, screeching and fighting. It took five men to pull her over to the pyre and tie her to the timber. Then one member of the crew lit a torch and Jane's screams and curses died away. She stared through the dark tangled locks of her hair. She was not afraid, only angry. For some reason, that frightened me. I drew closer to Teddy.

"We'll be givin' ye just one chance to save yer life," the torch-bearing man said.

"Will you now?" Jane said.

"There be magic in yer song. Ye sing us out o' this ice, we'll call it square," he said.

"Oh, I can break the ice," she said. She tossed her hair back out of her eyes and began to sing, a different song than before. This one was not at all familiar, and it filled me with dread. The crew did not like it either. Their nervous murmurs changed to cries of alarm; over what I could not tell. They bolted back to the ship, leaving me still bound and Teddy still unconscious. I stayed with him, desperately trying to rouse him. Then the ice beneath us shook and cracks began to form. The ice shook again, bucking up beneath me and sending me rolling. I realized with growing horror it was being rammed from below.

The sound of splintering wood filled the air. I managed to get my knees beneath me and scramble to my feet, turning to see a massive beast, a great white wyrm, rising up from the heart of the ship, cleaving it in two with its very body. It reared up higher than the mast, and I knew I was not seeing even half of it. The monster was covered in white fur like a polar bear's, fur which glowed in the rising sun. It was achingly beautiful; I could not look away.

Then it tipped its serpent head and snatched a fleeing crewman off the deck, impaling him on its monstrous teeth. His screams echoed over the ice, outliving him by several horrid moments.

"Teddy!" I called, running back to where my friend still lay motionless. But my hands had been tied behind my back and when my bootless feet slipped on the ice I had no way of catching myself. I fell on my chin and my mouth filled with blood. When at last I raised my head it was to see flames before my eyes.

They had lit the pyre. For all the good it would do them. The ship was rapidly sinking, the white wyrm snatching up all the men it could, ripping them to shreds but scarcely swallowing them before reaching for another.

"Jane!" I shouted, trying to rise once more. My head was spinning and the ice beneath me seemed to be tipping madly. It was only as I began to slide backwards I realized it *was* tipping. I rolled onto my back, trying to slow my slide with my stocking feet. Bootless and coatless, I wasn't going to last long in the Arctic, but a dunk in the water would finish me off all the sooner.

Then the head of a wyrm rose up out of the sea before me and I longed to feel the killing cold of the ocean. The thing's face was hideous, long and thin like a snake's with bulbous knobs over its eyes, as if its eyebrows were some sort of bladders. Then it opened its mouth to show me its teeth as long and sharp as rapiers. I closed my eyes.

Something warm and wet slapped around my waist and lifted me up off the ice just as my feet plunged into the frigid water. I opened my eyes to find myself safely past the teeth, which were rapidly closing behind me. I had one last glimpse of another wyrm plucking an unharmed Jane out of the fire's reach, then I was in the moist, warm dark of the creature's mouth.

The tongue, for that's what it was, released me. I feared I was being swallowed as the muscular flood beneath me sank down and the tongue pressed down over my head, creating a sort of roof. There was a horrendous pressure and both of my ears popped painfully. Then the tissue before me billowed out like a frog's throat. I was in a sort of bubble and though the membrane was cloudy I could see through it. I saw another wyrm with Teddy in its throat, then it was gone as we plunged into the sea.

We swam for some time through dark waters, and I was warm and apparently safe if not quite comfortable. Then specks of light appeared before us. As we drew closer I realized the light was coming from other wyrms. The bulbous knobs over their eyes were glowing eerily. There were dozens of them prowling around the wreck of a ship resting on the ocean floor. As we passed the prow I could just make out the lettering: *Erebus.*

My wyrm swam past the ship then turned back to watch the

approach of the other wyrms behind us. One lowered its head to the muddy bottom and opened its mouth. Jane stepped out, as easily and naturally as she would step out onto her porch at home. Her hair and nightgown were a constantly moving mass around her as she turned to face the wyrms gathering around her. She seemed to be speaking to them, although her back was to me and I could hear nothing. Then the wyrms began to move forward one at a time to present her with things they had salvaged from the wreck. She inspected them all but declined to take them, except for one small item, too small for me to see through the cloudy membrane.

The ceremony ended and Jane once more was swallowed by her wyrm. Then we were off, swimming through the deep. Once the ocean floor disappeared far below us there was nothing more to see, and as improbable as it sounds I drifted off to sleep.

I don't know how long I slept, but the nightmare which took me was a brief one. I was in a makeshift campsite out on the Arctic. There were very few of us left. Someone was cooking a soup. It smelled divine. I watched as the cook poked at the meat in the kettle, my mouth watering.

Then I walked around the boat on his sledge, over a little rise in the ground, to a place just out of sight from the camp. Something was buried there, but the wind kept blowing the snow away. I crouched by the mound, pushing armfuls of snow over the mass and trying to pack it down, but it was too dry and powdery and the next gust of wind took it all away. I could see what was buried there: a pile of severed hands and feet.

Lord help me, I was hungry still.

I awoke with a jerk to find myself face down in the snow. There was a splash behind me but all I saw when I looked over my shoulder were ripples in the water. My wyrm had abandoned me.

I fought back a sob of grief. What good was it to spare me from being eaten only to leave me to die in the cold?

Then I heard something clatter and turned to see a boat nearby, a boat mounted crudely on runners. If it weren't the boat from my dream it was another exactly like it. Jane had climbed inside and was rooting through it.

"What are you looking for?" Perhaps not the question I should have been asking first, but my reason was nearly gone. I could not see what she was doing inside the boat. All I could see was a bluish lump at the stern, a lump I became increasingly certain was a man's head in a woolen cap. A dead man's head.

"Oh!" Jane cried, straightening with a book in her hand. She sounded delighted, almost girlishly so. "*The Vicar of Wakefield*! He kept it with him all this time."

"Who?"

Still she did not answer. She looked at the book for a moment with a fond smile as she turned the pages then tossed it aside carelessly to resume searching. I looked about at the ice and snow until my gaze fell on another shape nearby.

"Teddy!" I cried, scrambling to his side. He gave a groan but did not quite wake. "We need to build a fire," I said to Jane, getting to my feet. I had been warm in the wyrm's mouth, but my clothes had not dried in that humid environment. It was with wet stockinged feet I crossed the snow to the boat.

Jane dropped coats and boots down on my head. She seemed anxious for me not to get inside the boat. I was suspicious, but practicality won out. I put on a dead man's boots and coat and went back to Teddy to do the same for him.

His eyes fluttered open as I lifted him, and he managed to sit upon and put on the coat himself.

"How do you feel?" I asked, peering into his eyes. His gaze was steady and focused, his pupils correctly sized. Something inside of me released a tension I hadn't realized it was even holding.

"Cold," he said at last, looking around at the snow and at Jane still digging through the boat.

"There are mittens in the pockets of your coat, I believe," I said to him, then more loudly to Jane, "we need to make a fire." I got back to my feet and crossed the snow back to the boat. "Jane, don't you realize the danger we are in?"

"Edgar," she said, pausing in her search to give me a fond smile. Fond yet sad.

"What are you looking for, Jane? Can you tell me that, at least? What could possibly be worth all this?"

"I have what she wants," Teddy said suddenly. I turned to find him standing, his hands buried deep in the pockets of the wool coat which was much too large for him. Then he pulled out one hand. The bulge I had taken for mittens was something else entirely. It appeared to be a fur pelt, rolled up like one would roll parchment into a scroll and tightly bound with leather cords.

Jane gave a cry and launched herself out of the boat, stumbling in the snow. Teddy took several steps back, tucking the fur out of sight.

"You don't understand," Jane said as Teddy continued moving away from her. "I need it. I can't return to my people without it. And they need me! They are dying without me."

"Your people?" I repeated.

"Selkies," Teddy said. "She's a selkie."

"Half-selkie," Jane corrected. "My mother was human."

"This is nonsense," I said. "Your father is as human as I am."

"Jacob is not my father," Jane said. "Penelope showed you once the place where she was born. I know she did, she told me. It's a place of great power, sacred to the selkies who dwell around Newfoundland. She was born there, she has a touch of that power to her. Don't deny it! You and Patrick were not the only ones to fall under her spell; you were merely the only ones she loved in return."

"This is nonsense," I said again, with more heat. But Jane could not be stopped.

"Penelope was born there, but I was conceived there. I am half-selkie because I am my father's daughter, but I have the power of that place in my blood, which makes me something more."

"What do you mean, more?" Teddy asked, still keeping his distance, holding the fur pelt close to his chest under the folds of his borrowed coat.

"It would take too long to explain. There is a war on, down under the waves. I am meant to play a part in it, to end it. I have the power to unite the tribes, only I cannot. Without my skin, I cannot remain in the deep for more than the space of a few moments. I cannot take my true form."

I heard a laugh then, an angry mocking laugh. I realized it was coming from me.

"Edgar," Jane said, turning away from Teddy to approach me, but I too backed away. She persevered. "I know this all sounds like one of Penelope's stories, and her stories are largely nonsense. That much is true. What will it take for you to believe me?"

I thought of all I had seen. Reluctantly, I had to admit I already did believe her story. All of it. But I couldn't bring myself to tell her so. "What about Patrick?" I asked instead.

"I didn't send him after my skin, I swear it. He chose to go in hopes of seeing a piece of that reward money."

"But..." I prompted.

"I did cast a spell over him," she admitted. "The same spell I cast over you. To dream of those nearest my skin, to help me find it. If you had ever seen it in your dream, you would have been compelled to find it and return it to me."

"I see. And Penelope's heart?"

Jane put her hand in her own pocket and took out a small metal box. This was the object the wyrms had brought to her down on the ocean floor.

"This wasn't on the *Erebus*."

"No. Patrick's ship wrecked in a storm near Beechey Island. But my servants have been watching all the ships at my bidding. All hands were lost in the shipwreck, but this they caught and returned to me."

I took the box and pried back the lid. It was indeed half a human heart. Blood and muscle, caked with ice.

"It was a foolish thing she did, tying herself to a sailor like that. But then perhaps I should not judge, for I let one slip away from me with my skin."

A look of nervousness passed over her, and she seemed to wage a war with herself on what words to speak next. "What will you do?" she managed at last.

I snapped the lid back down on the box and slipped it into my coat pocket.

"Penelope has been saved. Her heart is out of the sea; she can recover now. But she will never be whole without it."

"You're trading your sister's heart for your own skin," Teddy said. "Don't question what Edgar chooses to do with it."

"No, it's not a trade!" Jane insisted. "I can't go back to Penelope to deliver it myself. Even if I could, it's your right to be the one to carry it back to her. That's why I gave it to you."

"There's magic in it, I presume," I said. "I could use it to make her love me."

"Yes," Jane said, her eyes desperate. "If you put it in your own chest, she will be yours once more."

"I'm not going to do that," I said. The very idea was disturbing in too many ways. "She loves me with her whole heart in her own chest or not at all. I suspect not at all."

"And what of this?" Teddy asked, holding out the roll of fur once more.

"Let her have it," I said. Teddy considered this for a moment then relented, cutting the leather cords and unrolling the sleek seal skin before draping it over Jane's outstretched hands.

"Thank you," Jane said. "Thank you both." She laid the skin down at her feet and began shedding layers of clothing. I turned away for the sake of her modesty, but apparently Teddy did not. I opened my eyes when I heard his gasp and turned back to see Jane gone. Sitting in the midst of her discarded clothing was a seal of dark chocolaty brown. I looked into its eyes; they were Jane's eyes, with Jane's mind behind them. Then the seal gave a short bark and propelled itself over the snow and out into the open water of the sea.

I never saw Jane again.

Teddy and I were now alone in the Arctic. We scrounged through the boat for anything useful. We filled the pockets of our coats with foil-wrapped squares of chocolate and helped ourselves to extra mittens and woolen hats. There was another skeleton in the bow. This one was not covered with desiccated flesh, like the one in the stern. I tried not to think about the lack of flesh on a skeleton that couldn't be more than a few weeks older than the other, or the fact that the flesh should be gone when chocolate remained. I could not judge these men; I was about to walk in their footsteps.

We set out along the river. We had no way to make a fire, not so much as a knife to hunt with, and the chocolate soon ran out. We lacked only a harness and heavy boat to pull to be living my nightmare. Frostbite blackened our faces, and our feet soon began to follow. Teddy was worse off than I; the cut on the back of his head would not heal. Finally he collapsed in the snow, delirious with fever and too weak to go on. I settled down beside him and we both waited to die. I was not angry or afraid; I felt nothing but cold.

Why did the natives rescue us when they had given such a wide berth to the men of the Franklin Expedition? It was not because of Teddy; with his modern clothes they did not realize he was one of their own until he woke some days later and began to speak. Perhaps it's because we were only two, more easily fed than Crozier's many men. The fact that we had no weapons and were too weak to be a threat may have been a factor. I do not imagine the idea of all of those men starving nearby had rested easy with them; perhaps we were an opportunity to assuage guilty feelings. But I do not question it; I'm only grateful for it.

And it turned out that fashion sense aside, the captain had not exaggerated Teddy's skills. Once he was back on his feet he joined the other men in hunting, bringing home enough meat to feed the two of us plus extra to give to the tribe to repay them for their hospitality and later to trade for supplies we would need when we resumed our long walk south when the sun returned in the spring.

In all it was a year and a half from the day I left before I set foot on Newfoundland again. Jacob had passed on and Penelope now lived alone in their house by the sea. There was a look to her I knew well, the look of someone who has survived a major illness but still carries the shadow of death with them for the rest of their days, never quite recovering.

I gave her the metal box, and she took it with murmured thanks but held it without opening it, without even looking at it.

"I wonder," she said at last, "If I haven't been happier without this. No, not happier; more content."

"Perhaps," I allowed. "But the day will come when you will want it again, a day when you are ready."

She smiled a smile with no real feeling in it, a mere polite gesture. I realized the fire had gone out of me as well. I still loved her, but it was a different sort of love. It was the love of a fond childhood friend, half-forgotten. A sudden horrible thought struck me, that my passion as well as hers would return if she opened that box. Could I convince her to do it? Could I force her? I kissed her forehead and departed in haste.

So it was that a traveled to the Arctic and came back empty-handed. Teddy returned to Boston with me and became first my apprentice and then my partner. My life fell into a certain contented pattern, but the thought of the box still haunted me. Perhaps it always would. Some wounds never heal, and some illnesses there is no recovery from. Like Penelope, I would spend the rest of my days with the shadow of death falling over me.

TRIFLE

I t had been twenty years since Lady Enid had baked a cake; she hoped she hadn't lost her magic touch. After all, it wasn't every day that royalty visited. Enid had of course heard the gossip that the king was penniless and living on the hospitality of his lords, but such things scarcely mattered to her. She had seen the king's three daughters when the royal caravan had arrived the night before. Wouldn't a princess make a fine daughter-in-law?

Although it was not yet dawn, the kitchens were already hot and full of bustling workers too busy to notice her. Or perhaps they didn't recognize her in her plainest dress and apron. She found a small space at a worktable between a thick-armed woman kneading bread and a maid who seemed more interested in the young squire carrying in firewood than the tray of half-finished fruit tarts before her.

"I need your help," she said to the girl. "I'm making a cake. Can you help me find things?"

The tart girl pulled a face and was about to give what was sure to be a nasty retort when the woman behind Enid said, "Of course she can help you – milady." She never even looked up from her kneading. The girl dropped a hasty curtsy and scrambled to fetch the necessary utensils and ingredients.

Soon Enid and the girl had a bowl full of yellow batter between them.

"It's going to be a bit plain, innit?" the girl asked, still not remembering her manners. But Enid didn't mind. It was nice to be talked to like a baker's daughter and not the mother of the lord for once.

"No, love," Enid said, pulling a small glass bottle out of the pocket of her apron. "Not plain at all."

The girl peered at the bottle, trying to see through the dark glass. "What is it?"

"Winterberries," Enid said with relish.

"Oh," the tart girl said. "Are they tasty?"

"Among other things." Enid pulled the cork from the bottle. It was half-filled with plump berries floating in liqueur. "I'm not surprised you have never heard of winterberries. They only grow on a few shrubs in a meadow high up in the mountains west of here, and in most cases they are too bitter to eat. My grandmother was a goatherd's daughter, and she picked these berries herself by the light of the full moon on the eve of Beltane when she was thirteen."

"That makes them not bitter?" the girl asked, although from the look on her face she was really calculating the age of the berries in question. She appeared to be attempting to count on her fingers without actually touching her fingers.

"The liqueur preserves them," Enid said. "She kept the berries in this bottle until the day she met my grandfather. He was a shepherd who lived in the valley but had followed his flock up the mountainside. She knew she'd never get a second chance to get his attention, so she baked him a cake with these berries, and two days later they were married."

"Oh, it's a love spell!" the girl said.

"It's not a love spell," Enid said. "A simple love spell is just a momentary thing. It does not ensure a long marriage or many fine sons."

"Why are you baking a love cake?"

"Can't you guess?" asked the kneading woman, who had been listening in the entire time.

"You plan to marry the king!" the girl cried.

"No," Enid said with a laugh. "Being a lord's wife was trouble enough. To be a king's wife? I think not."

"Her son the lord has yet to take a wife," the kneading woman explained to the tart girl.

"Oh. Are you going to put them in then?" the girl asked, giving the thick batter another stir.

"Of course," Enid said, but she considered the bottle in her hand. The berries had been floating in the liqueur for three generations now. Just a dozen had been enough for grandmother to win grandfather's heart. They had had more children than they could count. A dozen more had brought her mother and father together, but Enid had only the one brother. Her dozen berries had landed her the finest husband in the valley – the lord himself – but only one son. Was the magic fading?

Enid made her decision. Using the corner of her apron as a strainer, she poured the liqueur into an empty bowl then dropped all the berries in the cake batter. There had to be more than three dozen berries in there she guessed as the tart girl stirred them in. Would that be enough? If it weren't, she could use the liqueur to make a sauce to go with the cake; there might be some potency in that. But how would she know if the cake were strong enough?

"Have a taste," she said to the girl. The girl dipped her finger into the batter and gave it a quick lick.

"It tastes more like wine than berries," the girl confessed, but Enid wasn't really interested in the taste. She was watching the girl's eyes, fixed on the young squire again as he crossed the kitchen with another armful of wood. He squatted down to feed a few more logs into one of the ovens, and the girl tipped her head to one side to admire the view, sucking the last of the drippy batter from her finger. The boy turned, brushing sawdust from his hands, and caught her watching him. He smiled at her, a bit nervously as if he were the one smitten and suddenly and unexpectedly found himself the center of his beloved's attention. Enid guessed that tart girl had been playing hard to get. Now she was slowly pulling her finger from her mouth to give the squire a smile hotter than the oven behind him.

"Yes," said Enid, "that will do fine." She poured the batter into the pans herself and slid them into an open oven. Then she left the kitchen to clean herself up. The king and his daughters would be up soon, and she would have to be Lady Enid once more, not Enid the baker's daughter.

She was still arranging her hair when the smell wafted into her room. She hadn't smelled it in more years than she cared to count, but she had never forgotten it. It was a berry smell on the surface, the sweetest and ripest of berries, but it was a smell that made your skin tingle the way it did after a good sneeze. It filled you with liquid warmth like good cognac on a cold night.

Mostly it turned the mind to all things amorous. And if it was reaching Enid's room, it was reaching every room of the castle.

Enid hastened down the stairs, the smell growing stronger with each step. Now, now that it was far too late, she remembered her mother's warning. Twelve berries, no more. But after all this time, how could they still be so potent?

She met her son at the bottom of the stairs.

"Good morning, mother," he said, kissing her cheek.

"Good morning, Alden," she said, a bit out of breath. She was not so young as she had been when she had first chosen the room atop the highest tower as hers, the room atop the highest staircase.

"You look..." he broke off from his intended compliment, looking at her oddly, and she reached her hands up to feel her hair, already tumbling down from its too-hastily done coiffure. She was about to speak when an even odder look crossed his face. "What is that divine aroma?"

"I believe that is my surprise for you," Enid said.

"You made me a surprise?" he asked, suddenly her eager little boy again and not a middle-aged man with too many worries and responsibilities.

"Yes, but..."

A loud crash interrupted her. Alden ran ahead to see what the problem was but skidded to a halt at the kitchen door. He was blocking the way but was too dumbstruck to move, so Enid peeked over his shoulder.

It was bedlam. Food and kitchen utensils were scattered every-

where, and there was more bare flesh on display than Enid had seen –
well, ever.

"What is this madness?" Alden demanded, trying to simultaneously storm into the room and shield his mother's eyes and failing at
both. The maids, cooks, squires, and other assorted servants came
down off the tables or up off the floor, straightening their clothing and
trying to look contrite, but Enid saw most of them were still casting
lusty glances at each other. "What is this madness in my house, and on
the day of the king's visit?"

"Oh dear," Enid sighed, recognizing her cake pans, quite empty
now. The bowl she had left the liqueur in appeared to have been licked
clean. It would be impossible to find the culprit, as the entire kitchen
staff had purple stains on their lips and... other places. It would take
hours for the initial effect of the berries to mellow, but it would never
entirely fade away. Enid counted her fingers. She predicted a surge in
births by Yuletide. "Oh dear," she said again. "They've eaten it all and
left none for you."

"What have you done, mother?" he asked.

"I only wanted to help you catch a wife," she said. "I was supposed
to hand this down to my own daughter, only I never had one, and now
there is nothing left..."

Alden took a deep breath. He seemed to be counting to himself.
Then he turned back to her and asked, "What are you talking about?"

"It was a cake I baked for you," she said, holding out the empty
cake pans, "to give to one of the princesses so you could eat it together," she said. "The winterberries are the secret. My grandmother
brought them down off the mountain when she came to live with my
grandfather. They are very potent magic, very good for making strong
marriages and... and many children."

Alden looked around at the disarray that was his castle's kitchen,
looked at his staff standing at attention but still casting furtive glances
at each other, then looked at Enid, raising one eyebrow.

"It was like the cake I baked for your father the day he asked me to
marry him," she went on. "How else does a baker's daughter marry a
lord?"

"Oh, mother," he sighed, running his hands through his hair. "Dad never..." he broke off, seeming to rethink what he was going to say, opened his mouth again, but still nothing.

"Your father never what, dear?" Enid asked. He looked at her, at the cake pans in her hands. He reached forward, brushed a bit of flour off her face that she had missed in her hurried dressing, and smiled at her.

"Dad never told me the story of the cake," he finished.

"It's not the sort of thing he would speak of, now is it?" she said. "Your father was always too serious for his own good, but I loved him all the same."

"Yes," Alden said distractedly. "If I post guardsmen in here to keep order, will they be affected by your magic berries? The king will wake soon, and I will not have him waiting for his breakfast."

"The smell will affect them, but it's nowhere near as potent as the taste," she said.

"I'll have the steward work out some way to ventilate this room as well then, just to be sure," he said. He sent a pair of squires to fetch the guardsmen and steward. The rest of the staff set to work cleaning up the kitchen and salvaging what they could of the meal. Enid looked about anxiously. She could not see so much as a crumb remaining of her cake, but in the darker corners of the room she was certain she saw movement. The kitchen's other inhabitants, usually well hidden during the day, had been drawn out by the aroma of the baking berries, it seemed. She wondered how many fallen crumbs they had managed to catch.

"And you," Alden said, turning his attention back to her. "I can win my own wife, mother, although she may not be a princess."

"I suppose you will have to now," Enid said with regret. "Full moons on the eve of Beltane are quite rare. And I am no longer thirteen." She stepped aside as the squires, under the harried steward's direction, flung open all the kitchen doors and began waving anything large and flat, anything remotely fan-like, to drive the still strong smell of the berries out of the kitchen.

"Quite," Alden said, his face twisting as he suppressed a rare smile. "Will you accompany me to the hall?"

"Yes, dear," Enid said, taking his proffered arm and letting him lead her out of the kitchen. She was hiding a smile of her own. The eager squires were indeed driving the smell out of the kitchen, out into the courtyard.

And into the open windows of the chamber occupied by the three princesses. Enid caught a glimpse of them within, pulling back the curtains to better fill their lungs with the rich aroma, giggling to each other as they grew drunk on it. Perhaps, just perhaps, the smell would be enough. Enough, but not too much. Her son didn't need three wives, after all, only one.

It was closer to luncheon by the time the king finally awoke, plenty of time for the cooks to put out such a fine meal that no one ever would've suspected the chaos that had erupted in the kitchen that morning. Everything looked just as it always had, and only the merrily breeding rats would ever notice the change.

THE ONMYOJI'S WIFE

enji stood, onmyoji cap in his hands, trying to lose himself in the gentle breeze that whispered through his favorite tree, picking up the scent of the peaches before tickling over his uncovered head.

It was divine, the sound of the leaves, the smell of overripe fruit, the coolness of autumn blowing down from the mountains. But it wasn't enough. It didn't dispell the memories plaguing him. Daichi's scream as the spirit flung him into the wooden crossbeam then hurled him down onto the floor. The shattering of bones, the tang of blood in the air. The malevolence of the spirit pressing at his mind even as he and Gakuto fled.

"If we could figure out where we went wrong," Gakuto said from where he sat on the walkway behind Kenji. "We were so close."

"We were close," Kenji admitted, "but it's hopeless. I never understood Daichi's ideas. Did you? We two could never figure out what went wrong." He left the shade of the tree to sit next to his friend. They and Daichi had started onmyodo school together twelve years ago, had spent nearly every waking minute together since then. Now they were a triangle with a missing point, no shape at all. Even Gakuto felt lost to him somehow.

"Every dead onmyoji increases the spirit's power," Kenji said. "I fear the wards will fail soon. It will escape the princess's rooms and take the palace."

"The imperial architect has been to see the master three times in the last six days," Gakuto said. "I think they mean to move the palace."

"The city was built to perfection," Kenji said, appalled. "Moving the palace would destroy the harmony."

"How can they not? We're powerless to fight this thing."

"It won't be enough. They'll have to move the whole city."

"We were so close," Gakuto said, burying his face in his hands. By his silence Kenji knew he was too tired to even weep, or afraid if he started he would never stop. Kenji reached out a hand to touch his friend's shoulder but then let it drop, afraid that small gesture would have them both lost in useless mourning and despair. He couldn't give in to that, there was still a battle to be fought.

Beyond the walls of the garden the sound of an ox cart's wheels on gravel broke the early morning quiet. Then they both turned at the sound of footsteps whispering up to them at a run. It was Naoyuki, one of the more excitable apprentices.

"It's Ienaga Fumihiko at last! It must be!" he gasped, but the grin on his face died away as he got a closer look at the two of them. Gakuto still had his face in his hands and Kenji knew he looked half dead himself, eyes bloodshot, cheeks sprinkled with the tiny bruises that were the signs of hard magic.

"Where is Daichi?" Naoyuki asked.

Kenji brushed aside the question. "Who is Ienaga Fumihiko?"

"The onmyoji who cleansed the governor's palace in Shinano Province. That spirit was much like this one. Fumihiko must know some secret spell, some new technique to bind this new kind of ghost. He's our last hope."

"There's always something else to try," Kenji said, repeating his sensei's teaching on reflex. In truth he had never been so drained of energy, so far away from hope. Death would mean rest at last.

He heard again Daichi's bones crunching, the splat of his flesh as his broken body hit the floor. The flatness of it had been uniquely horrible as it lay oozing blood over the golden floorboards of the princess's private chamber. He knew he had run away at that moment, but his memory lingered longer, watching the blood reach out, find the channels in the wood, spread across the room.

He didn't want to die like that.

"Come on, let's go watch him go in to meet the master," Naoyuki insisted. The grin didn't return, but there was no dampening his enthusiasm. "I want to see what he looks like."

Kenji was about to decline, gawking was the sort of thing the younger students would do, not a practicing apprentice like himself, but to his surprise Gakuto lifted his head, eyes glassy but dry, pushed himself up onto his feet and led the way through the gardens and dormitories of the onmyodo school towards the front gate.

The cart had pulled up and the occupant was emerging just as they arrived. A hand reached out to take the assistance the driver offered, and Kenji was marveling at the age of that fine-boned hand when the rest of the figure came into view.

A woman. A woman with hair shot through with silver, in robes several years out of fashion, looking around at all the palace buildings with awe and a touch of fear. Then she squared her shoulders and followed her guide to the audience chamber.

"I don't understand," Naoyuki said. "That is the Shinano Province seal on the cart. What does this mean?"

"It means tomorrow they start building the new palace," Gakuto said. The momentary surge of hope was gone. He turned to head back to their dormitory without a word of farewell. Kenji, suddenly more curious than tired, decided to join Naoyuki and the other apprentices in the back of the audience chamber.

Gakuto had been right, Daichi had been close. And if he, young as he had been, had been close, it was possible that someone else would get closer still.

If this woman was somehow the last hope that Naoyuki had spoken of, he wanted to hear what her plan was. Assistants would be required, volunteers called for. There had been fewer and fewer of those of late. Tired as he was, he would step forward. He wanted another shot at the demon that had killed his best friend.

Ienaga Chiaki, already on her knees before the ceremonial altar, collapsed, face pressed to the floor, and struggled just to breathe through the pain. It would fade; she knew it would fade. The burn sank deeper into her, loosening skin from flesh. The urge to scratch, tear, slough it off was thick in her brain.

But all of that was tolerable compared to the rage, the screaming in her mind, the thirst for blood that seized her throat, cramped her belly, demanded that she sate it. She was disappearing into it.

Then through the screaming in her mind, past her own tormented cries, she heard a tinkling of bells and remembered where she was. Heian-Kyo, at the imperial palace, in the rooms of the emperor's favorite daughter. The bells hung from a peach tree in the private garden and the wind that made the bright music brought the smell of over-ripe peaches with it. Chiaki felt squeezed, as if in the grip of an enraged octopus, her ribs creaking, ready to crack and pierce her from within, but past all that the smell of peaches brought her a hint of calm.

And calm brought her focus.

She managed a deep breath through her aching ribs, unclenched fists to press palms to cool wood floor, and summoned all she had left in her to focus, to make a prison in her mind for what was fighting to consume her.

Slowly the breathing came easier, the burn fading to a tolerable itch, and the malevolence within her was trapped, cursing in the back of her mind.

"Milady? Milady?"

Chiaki could hear the worried voice of the young onmyoji Kenji, knew he was frightened to draw closer let alone touch her. She stayed as she was face down on the floor for some minutes more.

She remembered the day she had brought forth her own son, a struggle that had lasted until deep into the night. When the sun had risen once more she had risen with it, her legs trembling, her face in the mirror blood-bruised and strange, a squishy emptiness at the center of her.

She felt much the same now, except not empty. No one could feel empty with a demon inside them desperate for escape.

"Milady?" Kenji called again.

"Don't worry," Chiaki said, sitting back on her heels but still too weak to sit up straight. Her hair around her was a tangled mess. How long had she fought before she had swallowed the demon? It felt like hours and yet the moon was still high in the sky, dawn far away.

"Did you do it? Is it gone?" he asked, still not drawing nearer.

"Once I leave, this place will be perfectly safe," Chiaki said. She could sit up further now, but her hair was still distracting her. So silver, when had it gotten so silver? That was what came of never going out among people, losing track of the details of appearance. It was terribly unfashionable even in her mountain town to look so old, and yet in the moonlight she found the silver strands quite lovely.

"That's good!" he said with audible relief. "But then Master Tadayuki had complete confidence in you."

Chiaki snorted her displeasure at the mention of that odious name. To claim to hold her in such high esteem and yet not listen when she pleaded that she was no onmyoji whatever rumors had reached his ear. Once could not both respect an elder and think oneself better able to judge her abilities than she can.

Chiaki felt hate burning in her heart, heat building as if someone worked a bellows in her chest. But of course that was exactly what was happening, damn that demon. It was going to find every way to turn her own thoughts and feelings against her.

Chiaki drew a shaking breath. "I will need aid to get safely home."

"Of course. The escort that brought you here will see you home again."

"No, I need you," she said. "I will need a trained onmyoji to help me with the binding spells. I can show you what characters to write but I need you to imbue them with power."

"Binding spells? But why?"

"Didn't you see?" Chiaki snapped, the demon pushing her to anger yet again. She took a breath. "The demon isn't gone; I do not have that power. So I have swallowed it."

"Can that even be done?"

"Clearly. If the bait is tempting enough. I guess I was."

"So I will help keep it bound until you reach home, but what then?"

"One thing at a time, Kenji-san. One thing at a time."

In truth she had no idea. All she knew was that her own death would free the demon, not trap it in her body or shackle it to her own soul in the afterlife. With her husband she had seen one demon drive entire families to suicide one by one. Throwing herself off a bridge would not end things.

But the demon kept whispering it to her all the same. The voice was so comforting, so persuasive. And she was so very tired.

———

Kenji expected a long wait to see Master Tadayuki but although his rank was lowly his task was an important one and he was rushed inside the audience chamber the moment he arrived.

Despite the early hour the master was already deep in discussion with two other onmyoji. They stopped speaking as Kenji and his attendant approached, the other two withdrawing to their usual stations along the side of the chamber as Kenji knelt low before Master Tadayuki.

"Report," the master said.

"The Lady Chiaki successfully removed the spirit from the princess's rooms," Kenji said.

"You saw it was done?"

"I was there the entire time. It was a technique I've never seen before; it looked like she swallowed it. I performed the usual tests afterward and the malevolent spirit is definitely gone. The princess can safely return to her quarters."

"Excellent," Master Tadayuki said, although he didn't sound particularly impressed. He cocked an eye at his nearest advisor.

"I do believe that is how she reportedly drew out the ghost at the governor's home. Her husband did the usual rituals with as little success as we'd ever seen him demonstrate when he still worked in Heian-Kyo, then she just swallowed the thing. The governor confirmed the story; the ghost never returned."

The master nodded then looked to the other advisor.

"It stands to reason a woman's magic would be different than a man's," he said after a moment's thought. "More receptive than aggressive, that makes a certain sense. The Chinese Taoists have studied the differences in the sexes, perhaps I can find the relevant texts..."

"No need," the chief said with a wave of his hand. "We are scarcely going to start allowing women in our order. This was a one-time special case."

"Of course," the advisor said with a bow.

"I trust you sent her home again?" the master said to Kenji.

"The Lady Chiaki had a request," Kenji said, trying not to sound as nervous as he felt. "She asked for an escort, a trained onmyoji to accompany her back to her village."

The master made a rumbling noise at that.

"It sounds like she wants to impress her neighbors," the first advisor suggested.

"We can't officially acknowledge how she helped us," the second said. "But an onmyoji escort is enough to start whispers and rumors. You know how women are; the intrigue is the payment she is asking."

"Can we spare the man?" the master asked.

"We don't need to send a good one," the first advisor said, consulting a scroll that Kenji took to be some sort of duty roster.

"She said she needed an onmyoji to perform a binding spell, I think of her own creation."

The master snorted his disdain and Kenji bowed lower.

"A new recruit would do," the second advisor said. "You could send this fellow. She already knows him."

"I would be honored," Kenji said, bowing lower still, feeling the master's eyes on him.

"You faced this demon twice in the last two days," the master said.

"Yes, my lord."

"And before that?"

"I was present at the first attempt as an observer." The memories rushed up like a tidal wave, his mind washed over in visions of the five most advanced onmyoji and nearly a dozen apprentices tossed around like a child's dolls.

"And you lost your sensei on another attempt," the master went on.

"Yes, my lord."

"Escort this woman to her home; you have earned that rest. We have much to organize here, but when you return we will find a new sensei for you."

"More apprentices than sensei," the first advisor fretted. "We will have to double up."

But Kenji wasn't listening. His heart sank at this mission that made him little more than a bodyguard to a very old woman. After years spent studying the theories and rituals of onmyodo, he had so looked forward to working side by side with an experienced onmyoji, learning to apply all he'd been taught. He wanted to study Daichi's notebooks, see if he could figure out what his brilliant friend had been working on. Now he was doomed to spend weeks traveling by ox cart up into the mountains, and if he was very unlucky he might get trapped there by the approaching winter.

———

Lady Utsusemi pulled back the screen of her carriage window to look at the thickly falling snow. She would have found it beautiful watching it from next to a warm fire at home. Caught out in it, it struck her more cold than beautiful.

It was late in the year for an outing, but it had been her only chance to arrange a meeting with her prospective paramour. She looked down at the poem in her hands. The paper was carefully selected, the hue of the ink complementing it perfectly. The perfume in particular pleased her, with its hint of cherry blossoms, although it was unlikely he knew of her personal fondness for cherry blossoms. She was ashamed to have such a common affection. The handwriting was impeccable, if lacking in a certain more creative flourish.

But the poem was vapid nonsense.

Lady Utsusemi folded it with a sigh. It was just as well this storm would block the mountain pass between their villages; she didn't feel inclined to even answer with a poem of her own, let alone extend a further more intimate invitation.

Although if he should show up at her window after trudging over the snow-bound mountain to reach her, she'd consider letting him in. If just for the way she could inject romance into the tale later.

The snow had a deadening effect on the sounds of the world around her. Even the crunch of the road under the ox cart's wheels had softened to a whisper. The keening wail that shattered the quiet calm nearly brought a scream to her own lips.

Could an animal feel such lonely agony? But surely that had not been human.

"Driver?" she called.

"I don't know, milady," he called back to her. "I don't see anything near the road. We're nearly through the pass; we'll be home soon."

"Thank you," she said, resisting the urge to tell him to hurry. She knew he was already going as fast as he dared. She looked down at the poem in her hands, now a wrinkled, torn mess. It deserved no better but still she was sad. There were no men worthy of her anywhere in the prefecture, it seemed. If only she could return to Heian-Kyo.

The cart slowed to a stop.

"There's another cart on the road, milady. It's stuck in a rut."

"Offer them assistance with my compliments," she answered, wondering which of her neighbors had also braved the darkening skies for one last outing. She hadn't seen any familiar carriages at the temple service. She carefully pulled back the screen of her window, allowing herself a quick glance.

She didn't recognize the insignia but the carriage was too high of quality to be local. What would anyone from the imperial city be doing here at this time of year?

The howl came again, closer. It sounded like many voices blended together, but all starting and stopping at once. The poem in her hands was now in two mangled pieces.

That definitely hadn't been an animal. It would be a terribly inconvenient time to have a demon problem; the old onmyoji was now two years dead and he had never taken an apprentice after his son had died from fever. Some whispered that his wife had been the one with real power but Lady Utsusemi made it a point not to believe in nonsense.

Footsteps crunched towards her.

"Lady Utsusemi?"

"Yes," she answered guardedly; she did not know the voice. Through the screen she could see he was a young man in fine, if now wet, robes.

"I apologize for delaying your return home. My name is Kenji. It's my cart your man is helping to move."

"You're an onmyoji," she said after closer inspection of his robes and hat. Judging by his youth he'd just joined the order and was on his first mission. "From Heian-Kyo?"

"That's correct, milady."

"How lovely. I was born in Heian-Kyo myself, but my late husband was appointed to serve the governor of this prefecture."

"I thought I heard the tones of home in your voice," he said. Utsusemi smiled. The fading of her youth was beginning to show around her eyes and mouth, but her true beauty had always been her voice, and that was undiminished.

"What brings you so far from home this late in the year? I've not heard of any hauntings in the area. At least not until today; did you hear that wail?"

"I'm escorting the Lady Chiaki back from court." Lady Utsusemi peered harder through the screen, but in the dying light she couldn't make out his features. He sounded so weary.

"But that wasn't her I've been hearing? The cries that wound my very soul? Whatever is wrong with her?"

"She is a brave woman," Kenji said. Lady Utsusemi pressed her lips together. She didn't like that evasive answer.

"She's brought evil here," she guessed. "Evil she can't control."

"She did a service for the emperor."

"Which I'm guessing means the same. And now the passes will be filled with snow and we'll be trapped here with whatever demon she's brought with her. I knew she would come to a bad end, thinking herself equal to her father and then her husband, both trained onmyoji. Now she's doomed us all."

"You forget about me. I'm also a trained onmyoji, and I swear to you what we have brought with us won't reach beyond the Lady Chiaki's walls." He had stepped closer, in truth closer than propriety allowed, close enough for her to make out his face through the opaque screen. The weariness of his journey added an edge to what would otherwise be a too pretty countenance. And his eyes were so very earnest.

"So you will be snowed in with us?" Lady Utsusemi asked, all thoughts of the demon gone.

"It looks that way."

"I know our little village doesn't compare to the myriad attractions of life at court, but I shall take it as my personal responsibility that you not be bored waiting for spring."

"That's very kind of you, milady."

She smiled, a more flirtatious comment on her lips, when that horrible symphonic scream shook the air once more. Lady Utsusemi would swear the snowflakes scurried to flee from it.

Kenji looked over his shoulder at the other carriage. It was out of the rut, Lady Utsusemi's driver jogging back through the deepening snow.

"This will test every bit of my skill," he said, not to her.

"Call on me when it is done," Lady Utsusemi said. "I don't think I shall be able to sleep until I know it is gone."

"I will," he said. "But you have my word: not beyond the Lady Chiaki's walls."

Those words stayed with her all through the night and through the next two days and nights as the wind howled around her home but never loud enough to drown out the tortured cries of Lady Chiaki.

———

Kenji put another log on the fire and tried to coax the flames back to roaring life. They didn't want to cooperate, the wood preferring to burn hot but dark. He desperately wanted the light. Lady Chiaki's home was laid out to take in the best views of the mountainside and valley below, of the cedar trees all around. But that was all hidden from sight by the storm. Now it was like being in a very small box surrounded by billows of wind-carried snow anxious to get in and freeze them both, bury them in a snowy grave for some unlucky soul to find come spring.

Lady Chiaki laid on her mat nearby, quiet but not sleeping. The quiet times were growing shorter and rarer even as she grew more and more exhausted. Kenji didn't know what he would do, but he sensed one way or another things were drawing to an end. The Lady Chiaki was weakening.

Giving up on the fire, Kenji turned back to the desk covered with scrolls, old texts and personal journals of Chiaki's father and husband, although some places had a writing of a different hand, one he was certain was hers. There was a wealth of knowledge in this house, experiments tried, theories postulated and mulled over, old legends carefully picked apart for nuggets of real truth. He could spend a lifetime studying the work of just these two onmyoji.

But studying wasn't enough. What was needed was skill, skill tested and honed. Skill Kenji might have a decade or two in the future but was just a shadow of a hope to him now.

Chiaki whimpered in pain, the sound as always containing the cackling laugh of the demon. Kenji knelt by her side, taking her hand. The nails were ripped down to the quick, a mercy since it kept her from tearing at her own skin.

"Milady, is there anything I can get you?"

"My husband, I need my husband." The words were all but inaudible, lost in the sounds of the demon, but she had said them so many times in the last three days he could have guessed from less.

"Your husband is dead and gone, milady," Kenji said, rubbing a shaking hand over his own tired eyes. He had tried to nap once. The demon had entered his dreams, had fought to hold him there. He had come close to not waking at all. He dared not nap again.

"Dead," Chiaki moaned. "Not gone."

Then the demon was clawing at him, teeth snapping at his face as he pinned her arms behind her. The demon was giving her inhuman strength but beneath that he felt the fragility of her old bones. It would be too easy to do her great harm. He wrapped his arms around her, hugging her tight and whispering the words of the binding spell he had long since tattooed on the base of her neck. It took longer each time, but eventually the episode passed. Kenji lowered her to the mat and stood up to stretch his aching muscles.

She had crafted a plan before they had even left Heian-Kyo. Kenji knew there was a reason she had asked for an onmyoji escort, more than the binding spell, but she hadn't spoken of it. She must have intended to show him what to do when they got here. But by the time they reached their destination the constant battle she fought with the demon had taken its toll. She had too little mind left.

Kenji returned to the scrolls, to his fruitless search, but the last words she had spoken came back to him.

If there was one thing she kept trying to tell him past the demon, it was about her husband. Dead, but not gone. Was that the key?

Kenji put another log on the fire and tried once more to poke some life out of the dark embers. He wanted light to think.

———

Chiaki's meaningful memories ended some time during the journey home, everything since then a fugue of nightmares that felt real and realty that felt like terrible illusion.

But this time when she awoke she felt different. The aches from repeatedly wrestling with a strong young man were as prominent as ever, the dry heat of her skin and the soreness where she'd scratched it raw the same. The demon was still there, jabbering to itself in the back of her mind, finding ways into her thoughts. What was different?

She was sitting up, that was new. Shitone cushions were stacked all around her to keep her upright like once she had propped up her baby son. She touched her face, felt fresh scratches crisscrossing the scabs of older ones, then short tendrils of hair brushed her fingers. She ran her hand over her head. Her hair was gone, cut unstylishly short as her husband had always worn his.

Just the thought of him and she knew why she'd awoken feeling stronger: his smell was all around her. She was wearing his clothes, the uniform of an onmyoji. The hat was on the floor before her; she picked it up and put it on her head.

"Is this right?" Kenji asked.

"Right enough," Chiaki said. "I need his box."

"Which...?"

"Under the floorboard, there in the corner."

Kenji followed her pointing finger, pulling back the mat and tapping the boards until he found the loose one.

"Do not give it to me yet," Chiaki said when he tried to hand it to her. "There is a spell."

"I didn't see one," Kenji said.

"I'll write it for you," Chiaki said, gesturing to the writing desk. He set it in front of her and she took up the brush and a slip of paper. Her hands shook and even when using her left hand to hold her right hand steady the characters collapsed on themselves.

"Can you read it?" she asked anxiously.

"Actually, yes," Kenji said, examining the slip. "It looks like your husband's writing."

"No one could read my husband's writing," Chiaki said.

"You could. And you left so many transcriptions on the margins of his scrolls I've learned to make out his scratchings myself."

Chiaki looked around the room, but there was no hint how much time had passed. She didn't even remembering arriving.

"The spell may take time," she said as he knelt behind her.

"I have become a more patient man these last few days."

"Has it been days? You sound years older, young Kenji." He didn't answer, just loosened the back of her robes to reach the crucial spot at the base of her neck where the binding spell held the demon. As the whispered words of the spell began she took up the box, the lacquer cool in her hands. She held it for a moment, remembering the day her husband had hidden it under the floor.

Then she lifted the lid.

Chiaki/Fumihiko opened their eyes. They could feel the soft touch of Kenji's fingers at the base of their neck, the calligraphy beneath glowing warmly. But that binding spell was no longer wanted. They reached back, brushing aside the young onmyoji's fingers, and wiped the tattoo away, flakes of ink falling from their hand in a sparkling mist that disappeared before reaching the floor. Kenji caught his breath but quickly resumed chanting the spell.

The demon sensed the spell's disappearance but mistrusted it, like an animal in a cage mistrusts a suddenly unlocked door. Chiaki/Fumihiko had to dive in after it, following it through the dark caverns of blood vessels, past the voluminous chambers of the heart, up into the palace of the lungs with its rooms open to the gardens of wind, screens dancing in and out with each breath. There they caught the demon, so easily, and carried it with them out through the gardens to the path that became a lane that became a road that joined another road to become the grand highway of Heian-Kyo itself.

Chiaki/Fumihiko coughed, forcefully blowing the slimy mass of darkness out of their windpipe into the box and slamming shut the lid. This spell they could do themselves, passing a finger over the latch with a whisper of words of power. The box shook and the lacquer grew hot, but nothing further happened. Nothing further ever would.

Kenji hesitated for half a breath but continued with the spell. Chiaki/Fumihiko closed their eyes.

Chaiki opened her eyes in a place that wasn't a place, although she could feel wind on her skin and smell cherry blossoms. It was warm, deliciously warm.

Fumihiko sat before her, a smile on his lips. He looked just as he had when she'd first met him, the young apprentice sent from Heian-Kyo to assist her father. It was a strange aspect to find him in, he had never noticed her when he was an apprentice and she was a girl of eight who was allowed to read all she liked provided she stay quiet and not disturb the work of the two onmyoji.

Chiaki reached up to touch her hair, hoping that she at least would look as she had when he had returned to her village at the death of her father. She had been an old maid of twenty then but that time he had noticed her.

The hair between her fingers was short. If fingers could see, she was sure they'd see silver.

"You look as you do in the world of the living," Fumihiko said, guessing her thoughts. "You are not yet of this world."

"Can't I be?" Chiaki said, looking at her scarred hands, touching the scratches on her face. "I'm so very tired. I fought so hard."

"I know. But not yet."

"You were with me always?"

"Even when you knelt before Master Tadayuki himself. He's his father all over again, isn't he?"

"He wouldn't listen to me," Chiaki said. "He didn't believe me when I said you truly were the one who always had the power."

"We went through school together, and worked together in our younger days. You can see why he would doubt. I never had power until you guided me to it."

"Nonsense," Chiaki said, but blushed at the compliment.

"Your father understood onmyodo like no one I've ever known in that world or this, and yet he couldn't explain it to others. His knowledge would have died with him, if not for you."

"Perhaps," Chiaki said. "I only made some notes. Found stories in older texts that explained things."

"You did more than that, wife."

"But now my life is empty," Chiaki said. "My father, my son and now you all gone. There is nothing left for me to do there in the living world but wait to die. Why can't I stay here with you? I've fought that demon for more than a month; as old as I am my body must be near death."

"I won't allow it," Fumihiko.

"But why?"

"You have a job left to do. There is an apprentice to be taught."

"Kenji? But he longs to return to Heian-Kyo. I don't think a long apprenticeship to the wife of an onmyoji will hold much attraction for him."

"I think you'll be surprised. He's spent days reading scrolls, trying to find a way to bring the demon out of you..."

"I needed you, but I didn't know how to reach you."

"He found a way. Clever fellow. And he has notebooks with him you'll really want to see, the work of one who would have been a great onmyoji himself in other circumstances. You might have misjudged him, his interests and his skills. In any event, you have the winter to convince him to stay. You and the Lady Utsusemi."

"What does she have to do with it?"

Fumihiko just smiled. And without meaning to Chiaki blinked, and the other world was gone.

She took off her husband's hat and Kenji stopped chanting the spell. Chiaki turned to look at him. The youth who had trembled in the princess's rooms while she tried and failed to bind the demon, when she fell back on the only thing she knew and took the demon inside of her, that youth was quite gone. Looking back at her now was an onmyoji.

"That was a spell of summoning," she said, taking the slip of paper from his fingers. "It conjures ghosts; not the ghosts that wander lost through our world, but the ghosts we hold close inside ourselves.

"Would you like to learn how I assembled it?"

All of the exhaustion fled from Kenji's eyes and he watched and listened attentively as she explained the characters that made up the spell that made one two-as-one.

DIN BA DIN

The freshly turned earth soaks through my jeans to chill my knees and I sit back, pushing the hair from my eyes then looking with annoyance at the mud on my palm now sticking wetly to my face. This happens more and more lately, my mind waking up about mid morning after my body has been going about its business for hours. It worries me.

A brilliant flash of light catches my eye and I turn to watch it climb the sky, like sunlight off a mirror, flickering but so bright. It glows too intensely for a star, more like the heat of a pinpoint sun. Lifegiving. But this sun goes up, trailing a long curve of white smoke behind it. I watch it shrink until it loses itself in its own smoky trail, far up into the blue.

Then the sound comes, a low rumble in my chest before my ears perceive it.

I look down at my hands, past the dirt. Sun-darkened, wrinkled, but not loose skin on bone. I'm forty, maybe nearly fifty. This isn't the rocket launch I dread, not yet. I sit on my heels, looking over my shoulder at the silent house behind me, perched between the road and where the mountain falls away, the back end on posts. There is a line of wash hung to dry, only my things. The children are gone. Forty-two at least, then.

I look around. A tray of plants sits beside me, a trowel stuck into the earth where I'd left it a moment before. Springtime, moving the plants from the greenhouse to the garden. I would finish this first, check the book later. On the days with no kids I don't really need to check the book, except to move the bookmark forward. Perhaps that doesn't even matter.

I dig another hole in the earth, pop in a curling squash vine. I like the days of long, quiet work.

———

I wake up to the sound of nearly hysterical giggling and I'm already tired. Devi's laughter comes in short bursts but Sita sounds like she will pass out from lightheadedness soon. I don't need to check the book first thing this morning, it's clear I'm in the five-six years. I pull on a robe and head for the kitchen. The children are at the table, each with a mountain of various cereals on the tabletop before them. Karan crams a fistful of his cereal mountain into his mouth, then follows it up with a long drink straight from the milk carton. Sita and Devi giggle again; well, in truth Sita never stopped but does cycle up to a higher level as Karan, cheeks puffed full and lips pursed to hold it all in, chews. Both girls have spoons at least and dig daintily into their piles as Karan passes them the milk. Arjun never looks up from his reader.

"Hey, Ma!" Karan says, wiping the milk from his face on the sleeve of his kurta. "We couldn't find the bowls."

"They're in the dishwasher," I say, not even sure where I'll start cleaning up. Apparently juice was had first; there is a sticky puddle running off my counter onto the floor. "Why didn't you wake me?"

"Arjun said we should let you sleep," Karan says. Arjun looks up from his reader as if just now noticing I'm there.

"I said we should wait to have breakfast. That's what I said," Arjun says in his crisply perfect diction. At this age he seems like the one who will always look out for me, but I know that won't be true. He will be the first to leave and the last to come to see me at the end.

Of course I worry if knowing that isn't what makes it true. Knowing how he will abandon me makes me different around him, I'm sure. But I worry more about Karan. How do I fail Karan? The pieces of that puzzle keep hiding from me. I don't get to pick the order of my days.

I take bowls from the dishwasher and set them on the table. Sita and Devi scoop up their cereal and put it in their bowls, Sita still having infrequent spasms of giggles like the hiccups. Arjun sets his reader aside and fills his own bowl. Karan puts the last two fistfuls of his cereal in his mouth and shakes his head when I offer him his bowl, determined to finish what he started.

"Don't choke," I say halfheartedly, then go out to the living room where the Din Ba Din book is kept to advance the page another day.

———

I'm too old to get out of bed. I had thought that would be restful but it isn't. I prefer to be working. Not hard labor, just to have some mean-ingful task so at the end of the day I know I did something. I find the control for the bed and sit up enough to see out the window. Even though I was just there yesterday I miss my mountain home.

The nurse left my door ajar and I can hear my daughters talking in the hall. They take turns watching over me, always one of them there, and this is a shift change.

"It was another bad one," Devi says. She sounds exhausted and I feel bad, although I don't remember the night before. "She was very upset."

"Asking about Karan? Those are the worst. Why all this sudden grief over Karan?"

"Sita, I don't think she remembers what happened to him. It's like she suddenly realized he isn't here."

"After four decades?"

"She's very confused."

"Well, that's nothing new," Sita says, so low I can barely hear her.

"Sita," Devi chides. "She still reads her book a page a day. I think that helps."

"I think it makes it worse," Sita says. "It's an illusion masking just how confused she's always been."

"Oh, leave her alone," Devi says. "She's had a hard life."

"It falls on a curve," Sita says unkindly, but when she comes in the door she's all warm smiles and words of comfort. I let her have her charade.

I remember what happened to Karan. I remember being told, more than once. My grief is scattered across my life. But I have yet to live that day.

———

Another rocket arcs across the sky. I always stop what I'm doing to watch, go outside even in the deepest of cold. I usually know it's not the one. I know when it will happen, or when it has happened, and I can tell if I'm about that age. I've been through a few where I wasn't sure, heart pounding long after the contrail fades from the blue sky. This is not one of those days. I can hear the kids in the house, Sita and Devi talking together as they do homework at the table, Arjun no doubt with them but silent. Karan could be anywhere.

The kids think I do this because of their father. They are teenagers before Sita works out that it doesn't make sense. The returning shuttles can't land at our space port, ringed by mountains as it is. They land hundreds of kilometers south of here and their father travels home by the mag-lev. Why would I be watching rockets launch when their father is already up in space?

Sometimes older Sita seems to understand me so well I think I must have told her everything at some point. But she doesn't let on.

Karan troops up the mountain, pushing a bike with a very bent front wheel, nose bleeding freely. Despite all this he greets me with a huge grin.

"I was watching the rocket, not the road," he says, not at all ashamed. "Someday I'm going up there like Dad."

Somehow, somehow I muster a smile in response. "You have to study hard if you want to be an astronaut. You have to do your own math homework, not trick your little sisters into doing it for you."

"You don't think that shows my teamwork skills?"

Then I do laugh, and bring him inside to help him clean up.

I spend a day alone, putting up preserves although the shelves are still half-full of last year's jars. Then I spend another day old, this time very old; I nap a lot.

Then comes one of the rarest days of all, days when my husband is home. I cherish those.

No matter when I am, each morning I take my cup of coffee to the living room and the little nook I've set aside for the Din Ba Din book. It's a single-file reader with an oversized screen in a decorative frame, designed to look like a large book lying open on a stand resting on a simple carpet on the floor. My father had gifted it to me the day I was born and every morning would spend a few minutes holding me and reading aloud my text for the day, then setting me on his lap and helping me read aloud. In the evening we would go back to the page and write what had happened that day on the bottom of the page using the elaborate stylus shaped like a silver plume. I rebelled as a teenager and refused to keep up the ritual but he turned the pages for me. When I married and moved away I fell back into the habit of reading the pages, missing my father so acutely, but not the writing. It was meant to be a participatory experience, but I no longer wanted to participate. I didn't even heed what I read. I stopped trying to match my clothing and food choices to the dictates of the text when I was eight. But I always read the page and think of my father.

I'm not sure when I awake how old I am and head out to the kitchen to make coffee. I can see textbooks ready for school, but only two stacks. The boys are at college already, the girls still a year away. I bring my coffee to the book and quickly do the math. Day 14278, I am thirty-nine. Devi takes the bus to school but Sita, on the school race team and always training, takes her bike. Devi carries both their books. The boys came out of the womb polar opposites but the girls work at finding things to distinguish them. When they were five they divided up the colors and neither girl from that day on wore any item of clothing in a color that belonged to her sister. Similarly Sita drew the athletic straw, and her sister took the drama and debate one. They don't seem unhappy.

In the morning I watch the latest vid letter from their father and think carefully before recording and sending a response. For some reason I worry more about seeming odd to him. Perhaps because the kids have never known me any differently, I don't worry about them. But sometimes Mohit looks at me like he knows something isn't right but can't put his finger on it. It is hard. Even if I could remember what I'd done the day before, I'd likely done it years ago and the memory has faded to just a few images, leached of all but the strongest of emotions.

Devi stays after school for drama rehearsals but Sita comes directly home, bringing another member of the team with her. The road to our house is one of the steepest and even the two of them in top athletic form are wiped out when they reach the doorway. I'm upstairs putting away laundry. Sita goes into the kitchen to fetch water, leaving her friend alone in the living room.

"What's this?" she asks as Sita rejoins her.

"That's a Din Ba Din book," Sita says with perfect teenaged disgust.

"Oh. That's that cult thing?"

"Nice," Sita chides. "Out of all of the religions in the universe this one is unique to our planet, and you call it a cult."

"Sorry," her friend says. "My parents say it's not a proper religion, just a hodge-podge of nonsense the first settlers brought with them."

"They would say that," Sita says and the friend gives a nervous laugh. "I guess they're not entirely wrong. It's a lot of numerology, astrology, and other fortune telling nonsense. It's my mom's book, none of us kids have one."

"So every day of your life is a page in that book? And you read them in order? How does the book know when you're going to die?"

"When my granddad died he had pages left over. So I guess it doesn't, or when you die you still have to do what the book tells you."

"And your mom believes in this?" her friend asks in a "she seems so normal" tone of voice.

"I don't know. Maybe."

"If you get a Din Ba Din book the day you're born and turn a page every day, then wouldn't every follower be having the same pattern of days? That makes no sense."

"No, when they create a new book it's unique to one person and the numbers and colors and messages are randomly generated by a computer. There's supposed to be some sort of ghost in the machine that guides the process, although I don't think my mom was ever that much of a believer."

"That's really weird."

"It's a dying tradition. Like I said, she never got one for any of us kids."

I put the last shirt away in my husband's drawer and shut it, my hands lingering for a moment before falling to my lap where I am kneeling between dresser and clothes basket. Sita is right, that is how the books are made, randomly arranging predetermined bits of information. But it suddenly sounds so much like my life in a way I'd never noticed before. And I'd never talked to my kids about the book, always reading the page in the morning when I was alone. Where had Sita learned about it all?

For that matter, I don't remember taking her with me when my father died. Those are the last of my memories when my days came in order. The boys were not quite two, the girls just infants. Sita must be spinning tales for her friend.

But I am uneasy. Something happened after my father died, when my husband had hired a nanny for a week so I could go alone, a blessed baby-free seven days, to settle my father's affairs and sell his house. I close my eyes. I remember going to my childhood home, I remember the trip on the mag-lev, but everything else is a blank of days I haven't lived yet.

———

I awake on my bed but on top of my covers, dressed in the white gown of mourning. I go downstairs and the girls are already awake, or still awake. Their eyes are red, their hair uncombed. They don't have white gowns yet; mine is left over from my father's passing. They don't hear me come down the stairs, engrossed as they are with the news on the vid screen. Endless coverage of the disaster, but no real information yet. They are still debating accident or sabotage. Even decades later the sabotage theory will still hold many minds. I didn't really care why, I just knew my son was gone.

"Arjun called," Sita says when she does notice me. Devi heads to the kitchen to bring me some of the coffee they've already made. "He will try to get away but the hospital is very busy and he might have trouble getting coverage."

"That's all right," I say. I already know he doesn't come, not even for the service. He sends flowers. I assume he mourns alone; a twin is supposed to be a doubly strong bond of brotherhood, isn't it?

"Until they know what happened, all the spaceports are closed," Sita says. "So Dad is stuck up there as well."

"No vid letter?"

"Not yet. Maybe they have rules about that too," Sita says.

"They must or he would've sent something," I say. Mohit was often away, but when he was home he was every minute with his children. Somewhere up beyond the sky he feels every bit of what I am feeling. But how I wish we could feel it together.

———

I think wishing is what started it all.

It seems cruel, following that day of heart break with one of the really bad days, the girls just weeks old and the boys barely more than a year, walking some but not talking yet. All four sick and Mohit up in space. I think I'm probably sick too but don't have time to dwell on it, constantly soothing one child or another, more often two at once. I can see waves of heat shimmering down in the valley; as hot as it is up here it must be intolerable down there. Perhaps it's the heat at midday or perhaps it's the medicine but for a brief lull all of the babies are sleeping and I sit down, too exhausted to even cry.

I was pregnant when Mohit and I married. It wasn't planned and everything happened so fast. I went from being an admittedly spoiled only child of a doting father to a mother in charge of two demanding baby boys way too fast. Mohit already spent most of his time in space and so when we married he brought me to his childhood home on the mountain, where his mother still lived.

At first I loved it. I still do love the mountain. But the babies were born while Mohit was away and his mother wasn't much help.

"I already did this once," she told me the last time I asked her to watch the babies so I could take a shower. "Seven babies one after another, two decades of my life went by in a blur. I'm old now, I've earned my rest."

I was angry with her at the time, as she wasn't all that old. But then she died suddenly just months later. Perhaps she had known something I hadn't.

But I think that's what started it all. Her saying she'd earned her rest, me only beginning to realize that part of why I was so tired was that I was already pregnant again from the week my husband had spent at home when the boys were a month old. I remember wishing a lot that I could have some of the rest I was earning at the time I really needed it. I wished a lot.

My father died and I went to my own childhood home. I remember a train ride. I have images, memories of a dream, or maybe things that feel like memories now but are really just fragments of that wishing.

I think I did something, that made my life like this. I can't remember. I don't think I've done it yet.

––––––

I wake with my husband warm beside me. I watch him sleep. A few silver hairs shine in his tight curls and even sleeping he looks exhausted. I slip out of bed and tiptoe downstairs to make my coffee and his morning cup of chai. I stop on the way to the kitchen to check the book, uncertain if I am at a moment before or after he retired, if he's worn out from his latest mission or if he is fighting the cancer already.

I don't even touch the screen to wake the display when anger invades me, not part of me but filling me, making my skin tingle then burn. I don't even pause to ask myself if it's of any use to blame the book, I just gather it up in my arms and march outside, barely feeling the cold wind that blows through my warmest robe as if it were the thinnest of negligees. I slip and stumble in my slippers over frosted leaves, finally reaching the fire pit already half-filled with sticks and branches. We must have had a wind storm recently; the fact that I can't recall such a thing just makes the anger inside of me growl the louder.

The book doesn't want to burn. It sits stoically as the branches around it dance with flame, dried leaves flaring up with a heat that strives to push me back. I stay where I am, although it feels like my eyebrows are getting singed. The leaves break free, burning fragments riding currents of hot air up into the sky to fall back down as ashy snow.

The thicker branches settle down for a long, slow burn and the book finally succumbs. The smell is toxic, melting circuitry and plastic. A few loud pops startle me. In the end all that is left is a misshapen lump and the anger drains out of me. I feel exhausted, but free.

In the morning I wake to four cranky babies, my own throat hot and itchy with a coming flu, my eyes burning hot in my head. Nothing has changed.

I pass several more days frightening my children at different ages with my unspoken despair. Sita and Devi fret over old me in the hospital, girls too young for school are carefully good until their brothers come home in the afternoon to take care of them.

Each morning I find the book and destroy it all over again. There is nothing else I can try.

———

I wake to the sound of the vid phone ringing in the dark before dawn. I sit up and turn on the screen, pushing hair from my eyes to see adult Karan smiling at me.

"Good morning, Ma. Did you forget I was going to call early?"

"It's launch day," I say, my heart sinking. The secret hope that I would never live this day dies.

"Yes, so I've only got a minute to talk."

I can't speak. I want to beg him not to go, but I don't have words he would believe.

"Ma?" There is a note of alarm in his voice and I realize I am weeping. "Ma, I know you're scared and you don't want me to go. But Dad has done this more than a hundred times, it's perfectly safe."

I've already tried to warn him, probably more than once. "A lot of things can go wrong," I say.

"Like the cooling system," Karan jokes, but he's naming the exact system that fails so catastrophically. So I really have tried to warn him; there really aren't words that will convince him. I wipe at my face. This is the last time I will see him; I don't want to say goodbye like this.

"I was going to wait to make a big announcement after the mission, but I do have some news that might cheer you up. Since you look like you need it."

"What's that?" I ask.

"You're going to think this is too sudden, so I'll remind you that you and Dad only dated for a month before marrying."

"You're engaged? I didn't even know you were seeing anyone."

"Arjun has met her once. He teased me no end; her name is also Sohaila."

"She's from the city? Like me?"

"She even has a book like yours. But there's more. She's pregnant. Two heartbeats, Ma."

"Why have I never met her?" I wonder aloud, but don't really listen to Karan's stammering answer. Why have I never even heard of her or her children in any of my future days?

Did I actually start changing things when I burned the book?

My heart starts to leap, but my brain charges on. More likely he had never told anyone else, and Arjun knew her only as a girl Karan dated once. If I didn't tell anyone else today, and the other Sohaila never approached us, no one would ever know.

"You'll meet when I get back," Karan promises but he's already distracted; someone is calling him away. The call ends.

I take the book outside and burn it yet again. I'm wearing white even before the rocket climbs the sky, reaching the point where I nearly can't pick it out, lost in its own contrail, then exploding, a bright flair then pieces arcing off with their own trails making a weeping bouquet across the sky.

I grieve, but it's distant now. Not like the first day I knew he would die. I weep, but I also know something I didn't know before. I have grandchildren.

Days pass. I dutifully burn the book as before I used to turn the pages. I wait, I hope patiently, for a day I once more wake clad in the white of mourning.

My daughters are still with me but I say nothing to them. I just slip out the door and head to the train station.

I've not been back to the city since my father's death. I miss him, but not this place. Crowds jostle me as I make my way to Karan's apartment near the space port and I long for my mountain home.

The landlord lets me in and I find what I need in his desk computer: her address. A few more blocks through pressing people and I am at her door.

She's not showing yet. Her eyes are red-tinged, her hair a bedraggled mess. She is beautiful.

She has no family, was uncertain when to try to call me. Karan had wanted to make a big announcement; she had thought herself still a secret. I don't know what would have kept her apart from us, perhaps her shyness, but my being here has changed things, I can feel it. It isn't hard to persuade her to leave the city with me, she likes it as little as I.

We talk and talk on the train, me drawing the words out of her until she feels comfortable enough to speak on her own, and by the time I introduce her to my two daughters I feel she is already my third.

She moves into the room that Karan and Arjun used to share. I leave her alone to unpack but she comes downstairs just as the sun is setting, her Din Ba Din book in her arms.

"May I set mine next to yours?" she asks with a blush moving from pink to crimson, and I realize I haven't burned mine yet today.

"Follow me," I say, taking up my book and leading the way out to the fire pit. She hesitates to place hers in the flames once the fire is going.

"This book is a tyranny," I say as mine hisses and pops.

"I don't really follow the directives," young Sohaila admits. "I just go through the motions for my mom's sake."

"Then what's stopping you now?"

She hugs her book, clearly debating with herself if I'm a crazy person.

"I want to tell the stories of my life myself, not warp memories to fit what the book tells me would unfold." The book, as if in reply, snaps loudly and falls in two smoldering pieces.

Sohaila strokes the binding of her book. "It's just a metaphor," she says. "A symbol."

"Symbols have power in our minds. Trust me, this one is a bad symbol." She still hesitates and I sigh, not sure how to convince her. "Life is a collection of days greater than the sum of its parts," I say.

Young Sohaila smiles at that and her book joins mine.

We sit together, watching the flames sink to burning embers and finally to cold ash. We cry together, missing Karan, but we don't speak.

Dawn finds me still outside, my whites wrinkled and dirty, Sohaila's head on my shoulder. The melted slag of our books is still there in the bottom of the pit.

My days have fallen in order ever since. The twins came, a boy and a girl. There are two of us caring for them, and sometimes a third or even a fourth as my daughters live close enough to visit often.

The book still controls me a bit. I rush downstairs first thing every morning to make sure it hasn't returned. I cannot count the days I lived, can't calculate if the future days I've already had balance out the ones I never got to in the past. Perhaps it doesn't balance, perhaps I owe days for stopping when I did.

I'll pay that debt happily.

SCI-FI SERIAL PODCAST!

Check out my new monthly podcast of serialized science fiction: THE TALES OF THE CHAI MAKHANI TRIO!

Elyot loathes the massive Commonwealth ships that hover menacingly over his home world of Adghal. He hates the Commonwealth enforcers who harass the populace even more. But with his mother missing and presumed dead, Elyot keeps his head down and strives to avoid notice. And he succeeds until the day two strangers enter his life...

New episodes of this sci-fi serial drop every 1st of the month.

Now streaming on Apple Podcasts, Google Podcasts, Spotify, Stitcher and more. Also available in eBook and print everywhere books or sold. For a complete episode listing, check out the page on my website.

COMPLETE SERIES: THE TRAVELS OF SCOUT SHANNON

The complete six-book series THE TRAVELS OF SCOUT SHANNON begin with book one, Under Falling Skies.

Scout Shannon's whole family died the day the Space Farers dropped an asteroid on their domed city. Now she lives alone, out in the wild with only her dogs for company. She prefers it that way.

But Scout finds herself at a crossroads. One road leads back to a quiet life snug under the protective dome of a city. The other road leads to a life in the rebellion, a life of adventure and excitement but also danger. Dare she try to find the rebels hiding in the hills?

Then a chance encounter with a stranger from the other side of the galaxy threatens to derail what remains of Scout's life. The entire galaxy awaits her, if she survives the next four days.

"Under Falling Skies", a young adult science fiction novel, set on a remote planet with a distinctly Old West feel. For fans of gunslinging women and young girl assassins. And dogs.

Under Falling Skies, the first book in THE TRAVELS OF SCOUT SHANNON, available everywhere now.

NEW SERIES: THE RITCHIE AND FITZ SCI-FI MURDER MYSTERIES

The Ritchie and Fitz Sci-Fi Murder Mysteries starts with Murder on the Intergalactic Railway.

For Murdina Ritchie, acceptance at the Oymyakon Foreign Service Academy means one last chance at her dream of becoming a diplomat for the Union of Free Worlds. For Shackleton Fitz IV, it represents his last chance not to fail out of military service entirely.

Strange that fate should throw them together now, among the last group of students admitted after the start of the semester. They had once shared the strongest of friendships. But that all ended a long time ago.

But when an insufferable but politically important woman turns up murdered, the two agree to put their differences aside and work together to solve the case.

Because the murderer might strike again. But more importantly, solving a murder would just have to impress the dour colonel who clearly thinks neither of them belong at his academy.

Murder on the Intergalactic Railway, the first book in the Ritchie and Fitz Sci-Fi Murder Mysteries.

ALSO FROM RATATOSKR PRESS

Also from Ratatoskr Press, The Witches Three Cozy Mystery Series by Cate Martin, a mix of mystery and magic that begins with Book 1: Charm School.

Amanda Clarke thinks of herself as perfectly ordinary in every way. Just a small-town girl who serves breakfast all day in a little diner nestled next to the highway, nothing but dairy farms for miles around. She fits in there.

But then an old woman she never met dies, and Amanda was named in her will. Now Amanda packs a bag and heads to the big city, to Miss Zenobia Weekes' Charm School for Exceptional Young Ladies. And it's not in just any neighborhood. No, she finds herself on Summit Avenue in St. Paul, a street lined with gorgeous old houses, the former homes of lumber barons, railroad millionaires, even the writer F. Scott Fitzgerald. Why, Amanda can practically hear the jazz music still playing across the decades.

Scratch that. The music really, literally, still plays in the backyard of the charm school. Because the house stretches across time itself. Without a witch to protect this tear in the fabric of the world, anything can spill over. Like music.

Or like murder.

The complete series is out now, and it all starts with Charm School.

FREE EBOOK!

Like exclusive, free content?

To get two prequel short stories to THE RITCHIE AND FITZ SCI-FI MURDER MYSTERIES as well as a bonus prequel novelette to the completed six-book series THE TRAVELS OF SCOUT SHANNON, signup for my monthly newsletter at KateMacLeodWrites.com.

Thank you!

ABOUT THE AUTHOR

Photograph © 2016 Jonathan Conklin

Kate MacLeod has written stories which have appeared in Analog, Strange Horizons and Mythic Delirium, among other places. She is also the author of two young adult science fictions series: The Travels of Scout Shannon, and The Ritchie and Fitz Sci-Fi Murder Mysteries. She also contributes to a serialized science fiction podcast called The Tales of the Chai Makhani Trio. She currently lives in Minneapolis, Minnesota.

Find out more about the author and sign up for her newsletter at KateMacLeodWrites.com.

ALSO BY KATE MACLEOD

Novels

The Slums of the Solar System:

Mitwa

The Mars of Malcontents

The Whole World for Each

Books 1-3 Box Set

The Travels of Scout Shannon:

Under Falling Skies

In Quaking Hills

Among Treacherous Stars

Against Impassable Barriers

Over Freezing Altitudes

At Galactic Central

The Travels of Scout Shannon Books 1-3

The Travels of Scout Shannon Books 4-6

The Travels of Scout Shannon Books 1-6

The Ritchie and Fitz Sci-Fi Murder Mysteries:

Murder on the Intergalactic Railway

Murder in the Skies

Body in the Catacombs

Death on the Summit

An Undiplomatic Murder

A Lethal Betrayal

Sci-Fi Novellas

The Intergenerational Tree

I Rise into a Daybreak

Caper Novellas

The Third Pole Job

The Twelve Days of Christmas Job

10-Story Collections

Tales of Blood and Ink

Tales of Old Gods and New

5-Story Collections

Tales from Heian-Kyo and Others

Tales from the Edges and Ends

Tales from Forgotten Days

Tales from Ancient and Future Times

Tales From Across Space

www.ingramcontent.com/pod-product-compliance
Lightning Source LLC
Chambersburg PA
CBHW032009180726
48283CB00008B/2598